VERA DAY

When Did We Lose Sylvia?
by
Vera Day

Copyright © 2023 by Vera Day
Published by Gordian Books, an imprint of Winged Publications

Editor: Cynthia Hickey
Book Design by Winged Publications

All rights reserved. No part of this publication may be reproduced, stored in a retrieval system, or transmitted in any form or by any means—electronic, mechanical, photocopying, recording, or otherwise—without the prior written permission of the publisher. The only exception is brief quotations in printed reviews. Piracy is illegal. Thank you for respecting the hard work of this author.

This book is a work of fiction. Names, characters, Places, incidents, and dialogues are either products of the author's imagination or used fictitiously.

Any resemblance to actual persons, living or dead, or events is coincidental. Scripture quotations from The Authorized (King James) Version.

Fiction and Literature: Cozy Mystery

ISBN-13: 978-1-959788-74-4

i

Chapter 1

Our love is like a sticky candy wrapper.

Betty Bell stood at the front of the classroom, immersed in scents of fruity shampoo, artificially flavored bubblegum, and high school jock sweat. "Welcome to the first day of our summer enrichment poetry class," Betty Bell said to her two dozen teen students. As a real live, award-winning, and practically famous poet, Betty Bell was the local celebrity of Tulip, Texas, and perfect, Deputy Miller had claimed, for keeping the kids out of trouble on restless Saturdays.

"You're not a *real* teacher," said Julie in the front row. Betty was acquainted with Julie's mom and had known Julie since she was a baby. Julie wore a cheerleader tee shirt, *Go Bulldogs!* and her glossy, blonde hair fell about her shoulders. She popped a bubble gum bubble. The rest of the front row, all girls, and all cheerleaders if Betty wasn't mistaken, giggled, though the young lady with box braids also narrowed her eyes and cast a glance at Julie.

Betty's mouth had gone dry. She shifted her weight from one foot to the other and back again. "And this isn't a real class, Julie. It's a summer poetry seminar to–"

"To help us losers get in touch with our feelings," said Hank from the third row. He drew out *feelings* in a long screech as if imitating a train with its brakes on. Everyone in Tulip knew Hank Young. At six-five and two-eighty, he was the star lineman on the Tulip High School football team.

This time all the kids laughed.

Almost all the kids, that is. A strikingly pale figure slouched in the back corner. It was supposed to hit 104 degrees this afternoon, but the student was covered in an all-black tangle of cargo pants, turtleneck, and long hair. Whether the Gothic soul was a girl or a boy was yet to be determined.

Perhaps it's a vampire. Betty fought hard to keep a straight face.

"Hey, Teach," Hank said, "aren't you the one who found the dead body?"

A trio of young men in the second row had pushed their desks together. One of them was whispering to the others in Spanish, pausing and looking up at Betty, then turning and whispering again. Betty fidgeted with her watch. Her Spanish wasn't all that good.

"Well?" asked Hank. "Was it you who found the dead guy?"

Betty Bell crossed her arms, trying to project more authority than she felt. "It's *Mrs. Bell*, young man, not *Teach*." A grasshopper knocked on the window as if trying to get in while Betty would do anything at this point to get out. "It was my back yard, yes, but it was

Deputy Miller who found the body. *The Tulip Times* covered the story."

"The newspaper?" Julie scrunched her face.

The freckled girl sitting next to Julie likewise scrunched her face and said, "No one reads the newspaper anymore. That's for old people."

Betty pictured this morning's edition spread out on the kitchen table at home, complete with coffee rings (hers) and inked crossword (her husband LB's), and she felt four gray hairs spontaneously sprout from her scalp.

"Oh, that Miller!" Betty whispered through her clenched teeth.

You're always pining for children to fuss over, he'd said. *This is the ticket.* When Betty reminded him of her failure with the babies in the church nursery, he said, *This is different because they're teenagers. The kids will love you, Betty. They'll be hanging on every word.*

The mysterious, black tangle of a student stretched its arms and yawned. Breasts, a girl, then.

"Are we going to do anything?" asked a curvy teen sitting at the end of the front row. She lived four houses away from Betty and LB. When the girl was a tiny, little thing, she used to ride her purple bicycle up and down the street.

Betty struggled to remember the girl's name. *My, she grew up fast.*

A lanky young man sat in the third row between Hank on one side and a round-faced teen wearing a marching band shirt on the other. The skinny youth crossed his long legs at the ankle. "The last teacher was better," he said.

Betty blinked. "You mean you've taken a summer

enrichment class before? You're Juan Smelly, right?" She thought she recognized Hank's gridiron teammate, a running back. Besides, who could forget that surname?

Juan pursed his lips and nodded. He had a touch of his father's ruddy cheeks and the rich, dark color of his mother's hair. "Three summers now, me and my cousins." He pointed with his chin to the whispering trio. "Jorge is too old to be in the class, but he's the twins' translator." Betty knew the identical twins' names, Santiago and Sebastian, because as twins they were a conspicuous pair around town, but she had yet to figure out which was which.

"Why aren't you their translator if Jorge is too old to be in the class?" Betty asked.

With a snap of his fingers, Juan said, "Because I only translate on the field, passes to touchdowns, passes for gain. It's rough, but I gotta be tough. It's the game of fortune and fame." He spoke with a rolling, driving cadence, like waves in a hayfield on a blustery day. Or an eighteen-wheeler speeding through the classroom.

The students cheered, and Hank gave Juan a fist bump.

Betty was losing them before she even started. She had to do something quick.

Standing tall, she announced with volume, "Words matter."

Julie rolled her eyes but paused her gum chewing. The Goth girl sat up straighter. Even the grasshopper at the window stilled as if listening.

"I know at your age it seems like the world isn't listening to you." She strode in front of the Spanish-speaking trio. Jorge faced the twins but had his head cocked as if listening for what she'd say next.

"I want you to remember a time when you felt huge emotion, but those around you didn't understand." She looked at Hank. "You lost a game, and your parents made you eat dinner with the family anyway." She looked from student to student. "Your dog died, and your neighbor said it was 'just a dog.' You fell in love, and your friends brushed it off as puppy love."

Julie started writing furiously.

"Hang on, Julie." Betty picked up a piece of chalk. "I'm going to make it harder for everyone." She scrolled three words on the board. *Flower, you,* and *sound.* "I want you to use each of these words somewhere in your poem." Focusing in on three words was a favorite technique Betty used in her own poetry. It helped her write a first draft without her mind wandering too far afield. By listing the word *sound* for the students, she hoped they'd use more than just the sense of sight in their descriptions as many beginners did.

"Excuse me, Mrs. Bell." It was the curvy girl.

Charlene or Darlene? I wish LB were here. He'd remember her name.

The girl pointed with her pen at the chalkboard. "What does that say?"

"You can't read?"

The young woman's face turned red.

"She means she can't read cursive," Hank said. "Me, either."

"I tried once," Julie said.

"It's pretty," the Goth girl said.

Hank gave the Goth girl a quick smile. "It is nice-looking, isn't it?"

Julie's nostrils flared, and she threw her pencil at Hank.

"That's enough!" Betty yelled. She already had a lower, slightly masculine voice that matched her height and athletic build. With the volume turned up, the students froze and appeared to be holding their collective breath. She snatched up Julie's pencil and placed it with a smack on the girl's desk. Betty was definitely going to strangle Miller. "The words are *flower, you,* and *sound.* Now write a poem!"

"Does it have to–?" Julie started to say.

"It doesn't have to rhyme." Betty's shoulders were tense.

"How long?" Juan asked.

"However long you want," she snapped and immediately regretted it. *I'm a grasshopper relaxing in the great outdoors.* "Just write a poem," she said with a calmer voice. "But remember the school rules." It may not be a regular class, but there still had to be some order. Betty tapped the poster next to the chalkboard, pointing specifically to number three since the kids were writing poems. The same, laminated poster hung in every classroom of the high school. *1. Punctuality. 2. Hands to yourself. 3. No profanity or lewdness. 4. Speak only when it's your turn. 5. Do your own work. 6. Cell phones off.*

The Goth girl raised her hand. "Is anybody going to see it?"

"I'll give everyone a chance to read their poem out loud." She looked at the rest of the class and added, "If you feel comfortable sharing. Otherwise, only I will see it, and I won't be judging what you say, just how you say it, to see if we can improve."

Juan slapped his desk. "You mean to see if *we* can improve 'cause you already the famous poet."

"Poetess, stupid," Julie said.

"Poet is fine." Betty quickly responded. She clenched her toes inside her running sneakers. Turning to Juan, she said, "You have a rhythm to your speech that I hope you can translate to–uh, *write on*–the page."

Juan's mouth dropped open. "I do?" The other students turned and looked at him. He clicked his pen. "Let's get this thing started," he said.

With that, the class settled down and wrote. Maybe things were going to be okay after all. But she was still going to give Miller a piece of her mind.

I love you, I love you, I love you.

Julie stood before the class, reading the final lines of her poem.

As we swim through life in our canoe.

She lowered her paper and beamed at the class, her gaze lingering on Hank. He sniffed and looked out the window.

"Thank you, Julie. You may take your seat." Betty turned to the class. "Thoughts, anyone?" She quickly added, "Remember to be respectful."

Jorge snorted. "You paddle a canoe. You don't swim it." He whispered something to his brothers in

Spanish. The twins laughed, and Julie huffed.

"An easy fix, Julie," Betty said.

"But did you like it, Mrs. Bell? Is it good?" Julie sat tall in her seat, and she was nodding her head as if urging Betty to praise her.

"If it says what you want it to say, Julie, then it's good. I have one suggestion, though."

Julie's face fell.

"Instead of *sticky candy wrappers of desire*–"

"You don't like candy?" Julie folded her arms and sat back so hard it jostled her chair. "Candy is sweet, but the wrapper is always sticky. Don't you get it?"

"Julie, Julie, Julie," Betty cooed as she looked to the grasshopper for moral support. "I just wonder if something like *thorns of desire* might relate better to your earlier line about the flowers."

Julie gasped and pressed her hands over her heart. "Oh, you're right! It's perfect!" Her voice was breathy. "Thank you ever so much, Mrs. Bell!" She immediately started erasing, rubbing so hard that she tore a hole in her paper. Letting out a barely audible curse, she flipped her pencil around to the writing end and wrote a new line in the margin.

The Goth girl didn't read her poem out loud, but after Betty dismissed the class, the black-clad student approached Betty's desk, her combat boots landing with heavy thuds.

A pale hand with fingernails chewed to the quick proffered a piece of notebook paper. Stanzas written in block letters covered the page. "Read it," the girl said.

Betty took the poem and slid it into her folder to take home. "You must be Sylvia Smith. It's the only name left on my roster."

The teen grunted some kind of noise that vaguely sounded like *yeah*. She smelled like she'd been working in the heat of the day and had tried to cover it up with overly perfumed deodorant. A tattoo climbed out of her turtleneck and up her right cheek. It was a feather, its ink ending in a sharp tip just below her eye. There was a jackknife-shaped bulge in the side pocket of her cargo pants.

The two of them were alone in the classroom. Betty was thankful for the desk between them.

Pointing her chin at the folder, Sylvia said, "Read my poem."

Betty glanced at the door. She considered making a run for it. Instead, she said, "I'd love to." Her eye twitched. She was a terrible liar. Retrieving the poem from the folder, Betty began to read.

One curse word after another packed the page. A violent narrative. Gory details. Betty had never seen such brutality in a poem, and that includes the time she conducted a seminar for a group of horror authors. Sylvia had blatantly disregarded the rules. And yet, sounding out the words in her head, Betty discovered the rhythm of the girl's lines and spotted a metaphor that was rather advanced for her age. Betty caught herself before she actually sighed with delight at the final lyrical stanza.

"Sylvia," she said, looking up at her student.

The girl chewed on her lower lip.

Several seconds passed.

"Sylvia," she said again, "this is–" *Very good, university level*. "Completely unacceptable." Betty's eye twitched again. She gave the paper back and heard a snigger from the doorway. Betty looked just in time to see a flash of blonde hair disappear from view.

Betty was a fast walker, no doubt a side effect of morning jogs keeping her middle-aged hips limber and all that. She had to slow her pace so she wouldn't plow over Julie and Hank walking down the school's sidewalk to the parking lot.

Jorge was already at his car, ushering the twins inside. Juan's dad was waiting at the curb. Other students mounted bicycles. Where was Sylvia? She had taken her poem back and quickly slipped out. The girl was certainly good at vanishing.

"It didn't mean anything, Julie," Hank said, his voice rising.

Julie delivered a punch to his side, her quick movement displaying the athletic rigors of modern cheerleading, but it didn't seem to have an effect on the big boy, or else Betty would have intervened. "Someone like *her*," Julie said, "can't hang out with people like us."

Who was Julie talking about? Hank's little sister? He'd been known to let the pleasant but peculiar child tag along to rallies and movies. An empty pit opened in Betty's stomach. She'd been the one as a youth who didn't belong, the oddball, the outsider, always the new kid at school because she went into the System when she was fifteen.

"I'm telling you, Julie, I was just trying to say something nice. It was just words."

Betty's fosters had been kind and attentive, all

three sets, but it wasn't the same as having a family to belong to. It wasn't the same as when her parents had been alive.

Julie spun and screamed, "Words matter, Hank!"

The county road on which the school was located headed south through ranch land then ended in a T. Turning left meant more grazing fields, turning right, the back entrance to Betty and LB's subdivision. It seemed rather silly to have LB drive her when she could easily walk the mile-and-a-half distance. She headed home.

The road was empty, the students long having driven or bicycled away. Cows bellowed, a rooster crowed, and somewhere in the distance a tractor rumbled.

Every place the sun hit her skin felt like she was standing too close to a campfire. It hadn't rained in Tulip in over a month. Along the edge of the road, parched grass sagged in defeat. The air smelled of dust and hot asphalt.

She passed a well-kept, small farmhouse situated close to the road with grazing fields stretching behind it. The band boy's poppy-red bicycle leaned against the carport. To the side of the house was an above-ground pool. A woman, presumably the boy's mother, floated on an inflatable lounger. She lifted her head and took a sip of her drink. Betty smiled. At least someone was enjoying the sunny weather.

Betty walked on. She often jogged this road in the

mornings. The two-thousand-pound, red bull belonging to a rancher whose name she forgot would stomp his foot every time she ran by. He liked to eat next to the barbed wire fence which sat a mere five yards from the edge of the road. His stomp was an earthquake that shook the asphalt. But this afternoon, he was way back in the field, lying under the shade of a thirsty-looking pecan tree.

This afternoon, in triple-digit temperatures, it would have been worth the silliness to sit in LB's Ford with the blazing AC.

By the time she walked up the driveway to her and LB's house, the heat had zapped Betty's anxiousness from her encounter with Sylvia and tempered her anger at Miller. She sighed. *I can stick it out for the summer.*

The house was typical for Tulip, a pale brick, one-story ranch hunkered down against the frequent winds of the Northern Plains. Big eaves acted like a hat pulled low to keep the sun out of the window-eyes. An old oak tree tried its best to shade the yard, but in the dry weather, leaves were sparse, and the tree functioned mostly as a whistle for the wind.

Inside, cool air enveloped Betty like a dunk in an ice bath. She almost gasped at the shock. Elevated voices caught her attention. Who was it? The only car in the driveway was LB's Ford.

"No way," LB was saying. "The Bible says–"

Betty sidled up to the doorway into the living room.

"Don't you start slinging the Bible at me, Lard Brain. Let me remind you of King Saul and the ghost of Samuel." Flora's voice. Betty's best friend was so worked up, her breathing was almost as loud as her voice.

Time to intervene. "I'm home," Betty chimed as she entered the living room. "Well, hello, Flora. I didn't see your car."

Flora Williams' real name was Wilhemina, but she picked up the nickname *Flora* years ago because of her propensity to wear brilliant, jewel-toned florals.

Betty felt a grimace flash across her face. She'd long ago realized that Flora wore outrageous patterns to distract from her ample bottom. The two women couldn't be any physically different, Betty with her lanky, lean legs, boyish hips, short graying hair, and plain clothes. Flora with her short legs, pear-shaped figure, a brunette dye job that bounced past her shoulders, and wardrobe colors that would make a peacock jealous.

Flora loved fried liver, too. Blech.

Planting her hands on her broad hips, Flora glared at LB. He stood stoney-faced next to his recliner and jingled the keys in his pocket.

Betty kicked off her sneakers. Strange that LB always wore shoes in the house, especially since he had cute feet.

"I came to see how your first day of teaching went," Flora said, "but LB here drew me into an argument about the spirit world." She pointed at Betty. "You tell him. *You* believe in ghosts. It's not all nonsense."

LB stopped jingling his keys and raised his eyebrows at Betty.

She shrugged. "It's true I'm kind of 51-49 on the matter, leaning towards believing. But I don't know, Flora. I guess I need proof. I need to see a ghost for myself."

Throwing her arms in the air, Flora said, "Only 51 percent? Well, it's better than Logic Bucket's outright denial." She brushed past Betty toward the entryway.

"I hate to see my two most favorite people in the whole world arguing over such a silly matter," Betty said. She followed Flora to the door. "Let LB drive you home. It's hot out there."

With her hand on the doorknob, Flora said, "It's hotter than the devil's armpit, that's for sure." Her face was flushed, and she was already sweating. "But I'm trying to lose weight." She slammed the door on her way out.

Betty leaned against the door. "She sure picked a hot day to start an exercise routine. LB, if she has a heart attack on the way home, I'll never forgive you."

He came up behind Betty and peered out the sidelight. "Oh, she'll be okay. You know how she gets."

Betty nodded.

He leaned in and kissed her forehead. "'Logic Bucket' is one of the nicer names she's called me."

An electron microscope image of an azalea spore hung on the wall behind LB's recliner. The spare bedroom was home to his G-scale train model. He wrote computer code for a living from the nook in the master bedroom. Betty turned and smirked at her husband. "I don't know how she came up with that name."

After dinner, Betty laced up her sneakers and grabbed her purse. "LB, I'll be right back. Just going to the grocery store. We don't have any coffee for the morning."

"You don't have to go on my account." He settled into his recliner and kicked up the footrest.

"Oh, yes I do." Betty cocked her hip and gave him a good staring-down. "You're so addicted to coffee that your eyes used to be green."

A grin teased the corner of his lips. He opened his book with no particular hurry and began reading. "On second thought, you better get over there before it closes," he said. "If *you* don't have your morning coffee, there'd be no telling what sort of beast you'll become."

She was tempted to flip the light switch off and run out the door, but even though he was teasing, he was right. "Love you," she said instead.

Chapter 2

In days of old, a device was worn
To keep your tummy nicely formed,
Now you'll earn many a chortle
To squoosh your waistline with a girdle.

Gravel crunched beneath her feet. The Tulip Grocer was conveniently located a stone's throw away from Betty's house... if a stone's throw meant traversing the graveled utility easement beyond her back yard, skittering alongside the fence of Petrol Pete's service station, heading north on the sidewalk for half a block, then jaywalking catercorner across Main Street.

It's been long enough. I need to drive again. The thought put a lump in her throat. "Someday, I will," she said in a voice loud enough to drown out the memories.

As soon as Betty reached Main Street, her mood lightened. She had fallen in love with LB's hometown when she first walked the central street's sidewalks.

To the left, the south, was a dining car from 1952 that housed a griddle and served cheap coffee. A little further on, Wanda's barber shop flaunted its original

1925 brick facade. Men gathered at Wanda's for haircuts and gossip.

Betty turned right. Boisterous laughter from Petrol Pete's one-bay garage flew at Betty like a feather caught on the wind, tickling and teasing her ear. Something about a goat in the house.

If she walked far enough in either direction on Main Street, she'd encounter historic craftsman bungalows from Tulip's boom years after the 1917 discovery of oil in Eastland County.

Betty crossed the street and paused under Midtown Creamery's giant ice cream cone, a vintage emblem in peach, seafoam green, and pink. She could see the Ivys' house to the southeast.

The Ivys' home claimed the highest elevation in Tulip, its ostentatious architecture and enormous size matched only by the moat surrounding it all. To be fair, the moat was just a ditch full of rocks to discourage encroachment of wildfires, but still.

Scattered on the outskirts of Tulip were ranches, windswept and dotted with cow patties, and clapboard farmhouses, weather-worn and love-strengthened.

When Betty approached The Tulip Grocer's square, brick building (a former girdle factory but perfectly adequate as a grocery store), Hank's bigger-than-life image in his football regalia greeted her via a poster on the glass door. *Hank the Hunk, Bulldogs' MVP of the year.* The poster would probably remain on the door until school started in the fall.

Once inside the store, Betty wandered the aisles, momentarily forgetting it was just coffee she came for. Why did she always get the buggies with noisy wheels? *Squee-squee-squee.*

She said hello to Juan and his parents in the diaper-and-motor-oil aisle. They were shopping with a newborn dressed in eyelet and lace. Betty turned at the canned goods. More families shopping together. A gregarious couple with four hyperkinetic children cavorted through the cereal aisle, the youngest child with thistledown hair. He was holding hands with Cap'n Crunch. Betty joked to herself that if LB died before her, she'd end up wandering alone through the aisles every day just for entertainment. She'd be a creepy old lady with a bunch of cats. Kids would egg her house on Halloween.

It'd be awful to be so alone.

Yes, Lord. She tried to cut Him off before He could nudge her. *I know You will always be with me. I just dread being old with no family.*

She stopped, pulled out a pen and paper, and jotted a short list. Might as well get more than just the coffee.

Betty jerked upright. "Oh!" she said.

Miss Mabel Lee, the eldest of the elderly Lee sisters and the owner of Miami Flowers, a misnomer of *Mabel Lee Flowers* due to the hearing loss and subsequent misunderstanding on the part of the sign maker at the time, stopped her shopping buggy and set her rheumy eyes on Betty.

"Sorry," Betty said. "I just realized I want my husband to die first."

Miss Lee's white eyebrows lifted.

"No, I mean, before I die." Her cheeks grew hot. "No, I mean before I cry." She sniffed and blinked away imaginary tears. "Or…" She dug through her purse and withdrew her package of tissues with a flourish. "There they are! I thought I left them at home."

Miss Lee took her rounded shoulders, swollen ankles, and non-squeaky buggy and made a U-turn then hurried out of sight.

Oh, for crying out loud. Why would I cry over not having tissues in case I cried? Betty's right eye was spasming. She should definitely never play poker.

It's just that Betty realized if she died first, LB would end up all alone. They had no children (not for lack of trying). His parents passed on eight and eleven years ago–they lived over on Coal Street–and his only sibling, an older brother, was way down in Corpus Christi. "Yes, it's better if LB dies first," Betty mumbled under her breath, "so I'll be left alone instead of him." She couldn't stand the thought of her dear husband all by himself, grieving. Besides, she'd had practice at being left on her own. She could do it again if needed.

Betty steered the shopping buggy with one hand while holding her grocery list in the other. Fresh collard greens and Brussels sprouts.

Squee-squee.

Whole grain bread, local tomatoes, yellow squash.

She rushed through the frozen aisle. Wouldn't want to be tempted by Blue Bell ice cream.

Dried beans.

The cool air of the freezer section seemed to have followed her into dry goods.

Coffee, steel-cut oats. *Squee-squee.*

Sweet coolness nipped at her ankles.

Whole grain pasta.

"Oh, screw it!"

Betty hurried back to the frozen aisle and snatched

a half gallon of chocolate-caramel frozen goodness, promising herself she'd jog an extra mile tomorrow.

On her way to the checkout stand, she heard Fernando's raised voice from the back. Fernando stocked goods and ran business errands and had been working at The Tulip Grocer ever since he graduated high school two years ago. His tone told Betty he was either angry or in pain. She didn't particularly care for Fernando, but in case he was in pain and needed help, she left her buggy and peered through the entrance to the store's back room.

Steel shelves rose from a concrete floor. The room smelled like plastic, old cardboard, and faintly of diesel fumes. Green-tinted fluorescent light gave the space a clean but unwelcome feel.

Fernando sat at a folding table. He was leaning over a *The Tulip Times* newspaper and talking on his phone. Sports headlines spoke of national golf and Abilene summer-league swimming.

Surely a golf tournament on the East Coast wouldn't spark that much emotion. And he was a young, unmarried man with no children, so he couldn't be interested in youth swimming.

His eyes were squeezed shut, and his face was red. "She did something real bad. *Real* bad. Ticked me off something awful."

Anger, for sure. Betty backed away and gave the young man his privacy.

Jacqueline Ivy manned one of two checkout stands. If Betty was (semi-) famous in Tulip for being a poet, Jacqueline Ivy was famous for being the only woman in town who'd had plastic surgery. Her breasts sat as high and firm as Julie's, Julie being her cheerleader daughter, the same breathless, love-poet Julie from Betty's class. Jacqueline's lips were so full of injections that they looked like misshapen sweet potatoes. She had hair big enough that NASA could see it from space.

Betty unloaded her groceries on the conveyor belt. "Hello, Jacqueline, working late today?" Jacqueline didn't have to work. Everyone knew she did it to keep busy. Her husband, Bartholomew Ivy, was often out of town, and with Julie being *the* popular girl at school and involved in numerous activities, that left Jacqueline all by her lonesome.

The plasticized woman simply nodded, and that's when Betty knew something was wrong. Nothing silenced Jacqueline. One time she got caught in a downpour between her Caddy and the storefront, and she chatted through her whole shift, runny mascara, flat hair and all. "Just God reminding us we are not washed clean without His help," she had told her customers between snippets of the latest town gossip.

Jacqueline swiped the carton of oats over the scanner. She was shaking so hard it took four tries before the machine read the barcode. Reaching across the red laser lights, Betty gently squeezed the woman's hand. "What's wrong, Jacqueline?"

Squeezing back, Jacqueline leaned in and whispered. "It's that new girl in town, the one with the dark hair."

"Sylvia?"

"Shh!" Jacqueline squeezed harder. Her Dazzle-Me-Orange acrylic nails dug into Betty's flesh. "Yes, her. She looks just like, well, you know." She glanced over her shoulder then mouthed the words, *my other daughter.*

Betty tried to pull her hand away. "What other–?"

"Hush up! It's a secret. *She's* why I dropped out of college." Jacqueline leaned even closer. She was the only other woman in town as tall as Betty, and while Jacqueline's proportions made her a Barbie doll come to life, Betty was more of a knobby kneed giraffe. The two women were practically kissing. "My parents wanted nothing to do with me," Jacqueline said, "when I found myself in the family way, so I gave the baby–a girl–up for adoption and went to work over in Abilene as a medical receptionist."

Things were becoming clear. "Oh, so that's how you met Bartholomew." He sold medical equipment to health professionals and had made quite a business out of it.

Jacqueline plopped back on her heels, her big hair bouncing. "Dear, sweet, rich Bart from the tiny little town of Tulip." Her gaze drifted to something far away, and she smiled, revealing her whitened teeth. Obviously, she still had affection for her husband of seventeen years. Or for his money.

"Does Barthol–" Betty started.

Jacqueline's smile faded. She dug her nails in deeper.

Lord, I know the woman's in distress, but this tug-of-war over my fingers is starting to get painful. Betty tried again. "Does Bartholomew know?"

Jacqueline shook her head. *Secret*, she mouthed. "If he did," she whispered, "D-I-V-O-R-C-E."

"Does anybody at all know?"

Jacqueline shook her head.

Betty had seen all of Miller's grandkids as newborns and knew that the little darlings came out looking more like purple alligators than people. "But how do you know it's her if you haven't seen her since she was an alligator–an infant?" Betty asked, skepticism tainting her voice.

"I know because… just look at her!" Jacqueline was nearly shouting. She slapped her free hand over her mouth and kept it there a moment. Then she whispered, "Just look at her. Raven locks, porcelain skin. A mother knows!"

Hmm, well, maybe. Betty had to admit that people didn't just fall into Tulip. They had to have a reason to move to this tiny town, charming though it was. What was Sylvia and her grandfather's reason?

Leaning on the buggy like a walker, Miss Lee pushed it up to the checkout stand, and Betty gave her a smile in greeting. Betty then turned to Jacqueline and, with a quick glance at Miss Lee to make sure she wasn't eavesdropping, whispered in the smallest of voices, "What did Sylvia say to you? What does she want?"

"Well, she didn't say anything, but I know. She wants Bart's money."

Miss Lee scooched closer. Maybe she was listening after all.

Betty positively yanked on her arm this time. Jacqueline held tight. Scanning all those cases of soda, watermelons, and boxes of cat litter had made the wealthy cashier as strong as a pipe fence.

"Now, Jacqueline, you've let your imagination run away with you."

Jacqueline seemed lost in thought.

"Jacqueline?" Betty was trying hard not to yelp in pain.

"Yes, dear?"

"If you don't let go you're either going to crack those fancy nails of yours or you'll rip a chunk out of my flesh."

"Oh!" Jacqueline withdrew her hand. She held her fingers up and examined her nails. "No harm done."

Class the second Saturday in June was pretty much the same. The rowdiness of the kids, Julie's theatrical gasps, Jorge's whispering, and Juan's jokes left Betty feeling more distant from the younger generation and more childless than ever. She looked for grasshoppers on the window. There were none. She soldiered on.

Betty explained the Japanese *imayo* form, a poem with exactly twelve syllables per line. Wrapping up her short lecture, she gave the students another three items to incorporate in their poems: distant view, sleep, and leap. She had given them an easy *sleep-leap* rhyme and wondered if any of the kids would take advantage of it.

Near the end of class, Sylvia offered to read her poem out loud. Betty tensed, ready to stop the child if she began spewing foul language and gore. But Sylvia's poem was about a blissful, sunny drive through the country. While she started with the proper syllable count for the assignment, she deviated at the end when the narrative turned dark.

Once slept, the darkness drawn, I leapt fools'
canyon grand.
Not right, but wrong, the night the theft.
Time swiped the moonroof, and now I see, your

auto-
Cratic love for me.
We went from bliss to being this.

"I don't get it," said Julie.

Darlene–Betty had finally learned the curvy girl's name–said, "Is it about loving the wrong guy?"

Sylvia wadded her poem into a ball. "Maybe," she muttered on the way back to her seat.

"Any other comments?" Betty asked.

"I like the internal rhymes," Juan said. "Like *right* and *night*. Plus she changed the tense of the two verbs you gave us, *sleep* and *leap* to *slept* and *leapt,* and they still rhyme."

Betty blinked. *The boy pays attention despite his joking around.* All the girls in the front row, save Julie, turned to look at Juan. When the freckled faced girl turned back around, her cheeks were pink. She drew a heart on her notebook paper.

Betty nodded at Juan. "I like the internal rhymes, too."

At the end of class, the students filed out, and Betty slipped the remaining, unread poems into her folder. Sylvia's black notebook remained on the girl's desk. Betty picked it up, intending to run after the girl, but decided in this afternoon heat it'd be smarter *not* to run. She'd hang on to it until next week.

A rumpled paper stuck out from between the pages of the notebook. Sylvia's slept-leapt poem. The girl had flattened it out and decided to keep it after all. How strange, the final stanza didn't even look like the rest of the *imayo*, and there was a weird line break in the middle of *autocratic*.

Chapter 3
Mother, my sorrow is a symphony
With minor chords and F-sharp fangs.

Almost two weeks later on an early Friday morning, Betty slipped out the door before the heat decided to get serious. She'd run even earlier, in the gray nautical dawn, if it weren't for the fact that wild pigs were nocturnal. As it was, she occasionally startled a boar that hadn't gone to bed yet. The snort of a wild boar was deep and loud enough to make her chest rattle and frightening enough to (almost) make her pee her pants.

So, she always waited for sunrise.

Today, there were no clouds, and the morning sun burned yellow-hot as she began her jog. Her feet fell into a steady rhythm on the sidewalk, and her thoughts drifted toward her students.

Class wasn't getting any better. Julie primped and exhaled dramatic sighs. Hank spent long minutes staring out the window. Juan's jokes were becoming vulgar, and Jorge's whispers were getting louder. Sylvia, apparently not as interested as she was during the earlier classes, doodled.

Betty's footfalls grew louder, a sign that her legs were getting tired.

Was Sylvia bored? Betty decided on a whim to make the next in-class assignment more challenging in order to engage the girl.

Betty crossed Main and hung a left on Coal Street, forcing her feet to land softer, springier.

Passing a fire hydrant triggered a childhood memory. She was a little girl in Waco, and it was just as hot and dry as it was now in Tulip. A main had burst, and the kids on the block played in the cool, spurting water. Betty's mother joined in, throwing her head back, laughing. Soaking wet. Dancing barefoot.

Betty missed both of her parents, but especially her mother. Folks said if her mother had lived longer, the two of them would have started to chafe, mothers and daughters often clashing that way. Betty wasn't so sure. Her mom had been playful and childlike, but hard-working and practical, too. There hadn't been much drama in the house.

I wonder what it's like in the Ivy household. Now there's a lot of drama under one roof.

She hung a right at Avenue G and passed the white clapboard church. Not Tulip Community Church where Betty went, but the historic First Baptist Church. "It's not hotter than hell here," said the marquee.

A little further down the road, Mama Teach's pink bungalow cheered the street.

"G'morning, Betty!" Mama Teach called from her front porch. She was sitting in one of two rocking chairs and thumping the porch planks with her walker. The walker and the new screw in her hip were byproducts of a sleepy-driver accident. The other driver, not Mama Teach.

Driving is dangerous. Betty slowed to a stop. "You're up early," she said.

"C'mon up here, child." Mama Teach was older than dirt. She was the only person Betty knew besides the Lee sisters who qualified to call her *child*. At ninety-something, Mama Teach was the oldest active educator north of Austin. She knew all the teachers in the district plus the seven surrounding districts, and they all knew her.

Betty obeyed, making her way up the front sidewalk, but she perched sideways on the porch stairs rather than get her perspiration all over the woman's other rocker.

"The kids miss you," Betty said, looking up at the old woman. "Especially Juan and his cousins."

Mama Teach waved off the compliment. "Eh, that Juan and his cousins are probably enjoying something other than the science experiments I make them do." She looked Betty up and down, frowning here, pursing her lips there, as if grading a lab project. "You look unsettled, child."

Betty nodded. "I'm not very good at this teaching thing. I thought I'd feel a connection by now, but I feel mostly like I'm babysitting. And the kids are so dark. Well, except for Julie. They write poems about death and parents who don't understand them. I expected this–they're teenagers, after all–but I didn't expect it to get me so down. And Sylvia, the new girl!" Betty propped her elbows on her knees and let her head fall into her hands. "She scared me at first, but I was wrong about her." Betty cringed when she pictured Sylvia's bold tattoo. "She has this huge tattoo on her face that makes her look like a thug, and her eyes dart about like she's expecting trouble. But she's also my brightest and most sensitive student with insightful reflections and advanced techniques. She probably hates me." Betty shook the image of Sylvia out of her head. "Then there's Julie Ivy. I'm not reaching Julie at all. She's rather shallow in her expressions. Juan jokes more than writes, mostly at my expense but he's got rhythm to his poetry and could be really good. Then there's–"

"Some children we misjudge at first," the old woman said, interrupting Betty's list of complaints. "Now take Sara Higgins." Sara Higgins was Ben's adoptive mother, the same Ben found dead in Betty's back yard. "I thought Sara was full of herself, but she ended up with a heart bigger than all of Tulip." Mama Teach stared off in the distance. "Bless her heart, she must be grieving something awful."

"Yes," Betty said.

"And I was wrong about Bartholemew Ivy. I never thought he'd amount to much. But now he has the biggest house in town, prettiest wife, too. Now that don't mean success to everyone. But for Bartholemew, he was such a schemer and dreamer, that I think seeing his plans come to life does make him happy. His plans and his faith."

Indeed, he sang alto in the church choir whenever he was in town. You could tell by the rapturous look on his face that he sang every note for the Lord.

The old woman stopped rocking. "Your first mistake," she said, pointing her arthritic finger at Betty, "was to think what was in it for you. Our summer enrichment programs are about the kids and *their* future. Second, if the new girl is as bright as you say, she'll see that you've come around. And Julie Ivy, now don't you worry about her none. People like her, as long as she knows the Lord, will come out on top, eventually, after she makes a couple of wrong turns. You just watch."

Betty nodded, too embarrassed to say anything once she realized she had gone into this whole teaching thing all wrong. *It's not about me.*

"How's Larry?" Mama Teach asked. "You two have any plans for the 4th of July?"

Betty perked up at hearing LB's given name. "He's great. We'll be going to a cookout at Flora's." It dawned on Betty she didn't have to teach this week because of Independence Day. Good, it would give her time to adjust her attitude.

Shaking her head, Mama Teach said, "That Larry, nerdiest kid I ever taught."

At the start of the first class after the holiday, the freckle-faced cheerleader abandoned her minion position next to Julie in the first row and moved next to Juan. Betty could tell he didn't hate it.

Betty discussed different ways to use metaphors, but she gave the students leeway to write a poem in whatever language they chose.

After Jorge's translation to his younger brothers, Santiago's left hand and Sebastian's right hand popped up at the same time.

"En espanol?" Santiago (or was it Sebastian?)

asked.

"Si," Betty replied.

Julie popped a bubblegum bubble. "I'm writing my poem in English, totally. English has the best met-a-phors." She said the word slowly, apparently having just learned it.

Betty had hoped this challenging lesson would appeal to Syliva, but Sylvia wasn't in class. *That's odd, when did we lose Sylvia?*

Chapter 4

shadowed corner web
silken silver labyrinth
tiny fangs tarry

"I'm afraid I've run Sylvia off," Betty said. She was talking to Flora on the phone and pacing the living room while LB snoozed on the couch. "She wasn't in class today."

Flora made a *tsk-tsk* sound. "I can tell your blessed little heart's in a tizzy. I'll be right there."

Betty stopped pacing. "What? Why?"

"We have to check on the child, of course," Flora said. "I'll bring my EVP recorder. It's a new app on my phone, and I've been itchin' to try it out."

"It's somebody's home, Flora." Betty's voice rose, startling LB awake. "It's not a fun house for your ghost-hunting expeditions."

Betty waited, but Flora had already hung up. Turning to LB, she said, "It seems to me if Sylvia's grandfather bought–"

"Rented," LB said, "with cash." He yawned and sat up. "He didn't buy it. Did you know thirty-six percent of Americans rent?"

"How do you know Sylvia's grandfather paid the rent with cash?" she asked, ignoring his piece of trivia. LB was all about little facts. He was a walking Google search engine. "Oh, it doesn't matter how you know about Mr. Smith's finances. The point is," Betty said, "if Mr. Smith rented a secluded house, then he values his privacy. We shouldn't go calling on him and his granddaughter unannounced."

He let out a non-committal grunt.

Betty huffed. "You're no help."

"Flora is your best friend, not mine."

"I just wish you two would get along."

LB picked up his empty coffee cup and headed for the kitchen. When he came back (coffee cup full), he said, "Can't you find another best friend? Jacqueline, perhaps?"

She wrinkled her nose. "That woman exhausts me."

"Then someone like Juanita Smelly or Pastor Bethany. Nice, normal people."

"Mrs. Smelly knows about the difficulty I had in the church nursery. She wouldn't want me around her baby. And Pastor Bethany scares me."

LB settled into his reading chair. He let out a little laugh. "Pastor Bethany is less than five feet tall and weighs eighty-eight pounds in a rainstorm."

Betty crossed her arms. "But she's intimidating with all her hermon... humanet... hermeneutics this and exegesis that. I can't pronounce the words, much less keep up with her."

LB started to reply, but a shave-and-a-haircut horn, Flora's signature announcement, sounded from the driveway.

"There's Flora," Betty said. She leaned over and kissed LB's forehead. "No, no," she said in a deadpan, "don't get up on my account."

"Love you, Betty."

"Love you, bye."

Betty opened the passenger door of Flora's older model Chevy Blazer, painted royal blue and mud, and late afternoon sunlight flooded the car. Flora wore a tent-size, empire-waist tunic that cinched her torso in its narrowest place--just below her breasts--and fell long and wide enough to cover her bottom. Sunrays lit up the turquoise and fuschia fabric like a disco ball.

Betty was wearing one of LB's tee shirts. Again.

Sugarpie, Jacqueline's miniature Dachshund, had a bigger wardrobe than Betty did. Nuns had more dresses. Sometimes Betty had to borrow LB's socks, too. But only when she got behind on the laundry.

Moving aside a plastic bottle, Betty climbed in. "What's this?" Betty asked as she waved the bottle. There were more like it, unopened, on the floor. She squinted at the label. "Grapefruit–"

"Grapefruit flavored water," Flora said. She backed out of the drive. "It's the latest diet."

"I thought you were walking to lose weight."

"This doesn't involve as much sweat. You just eat anything that's grapefruit flavored, as much as you like."

Betty frowned. "Doesn't sound like a well-rounded

diet. Besides, didn't you try the Grapefruit Diet in 2002?"

"This is different."

They turned onto the county road heading east, but then Flora took a left on Highway 6.

"Flora, this isn't the way to the old Sanchez–I mean to the Smiths' house."

Flora cranked up the air conditioning. Her face was blotchy. She really suffered in the heat. "The county is making repairs on the covered bridge."

"How do you know?" Betty's eyes narrowed. "You've already been out there, haven't you? You thought you'd welcome them to the neighborhood while you took a peek at the haunted house." Betty put air quotes around "haunted house."

Flora cleared her throat. "Maybe."

"Flora!"

She shrugged. "You know decades ago the youngest Sanchez girl drowned in the creek behind the house."

There was a cow munching away on the wrong side of a barbed wire fence. "Watch out for the cow."

"The cow's in the ditch. I'm not going to hit it."

Betty sent a quick text to let Charlie, the rancher out here, know he had a cow out.

"Anyway," Flora continued, "I was too yellow-bellied to go look for the ghost when the house was abandoned. So, I baked up a pan of my famous grapefruit casserole and took one over."

Betty folded her arms. "You don't have a famous grapefruit casserole. What did they say when you gave it to them? Is that pickup truck about to pull out?"

"The pickup driver sees us. It may not be a famous

casserole, but it is grapefruit. Grapefruit casserole is kinda icky, actually," Flora said with a sour look on her face. "Sylvia's grandfather wasn't interested in chatting. He wouldn't open the door and told me to leave it on the porch. Can you imagine?" She glanced down at her dashboard. "Oops."

"Oops what? Is that another cow out?" Betty pointed at a dark shape in the road.

"It's a blown truck tire. We'll get around it with room to spare. Anyway, now that Sylvia is missing, we have a legitimate reason to come calling." A light flashed on the dashboard. "Uh-oh."

"Uh-oh *what?*"

The SUV hiccuped, and Flora brought it to a rest on the shoulder. "We're out of gas."

Betty glanced around. They were in the hollow between Charlie's land and a pecan grove that Miller's daughter owned, a well-known cell hole, no service.

Without the air conditioner going, the car immediately started heating up. A sheen broke out on Flora's face. "I'm sorry, Betty. Honest, I didn't know I was low on gas when we set out."

"Oh, I'm not mad." She was actually quite concerned about her best friend in all this heat. It's one thing to be accustomed to jogging in the heat. Flora, on the other hand, spent her days crunching numbers in the air-conditioned offices of the A1 Synergy Energy Electric Cooperative which went by the unfortunate nickname of "the Coop," as in chicken. Trying to smile, Betty said, "It's only a mile to the highway gas station. I'll buy a gallon. Be back in thirty minutes."

Just don't have a heat stroke while I'm gone.

Betty grabbed the red plastic gas can from the

back—everybody in Tulip had one, it was part of everyday life in small town Texas—and climbed out of the SUV. She glanced once more at her flushed friend. If Flora did survive this little speed bump, Betty would have to smack her upside the head.

With an impressive layer of perspiration and a full gas can, Betty returned to an empty Blazer. She dropped the can and yanked the door open, bracing herself for the expected limp body of her friend.

The front seat was empty. She leaned in. So were the back seat and the back hatch.

"What are you doing, Betty?"

Betty bolted upright and hit her head in the process.

Walking out from beneath a pecan tree was Flora in all her beautiful peacockness.

"I didn't see you over there," Betty said.

With each step in the dry grass, a burst of grasshoppers took flight, their clicking wings combining to make a murmur louder and more deep-throated than any of God's insects on their own.

"It was cooler under the trees," Flora said, "even if they are half dead in this drought." She lifted a foot high above the sun-bleached stalks of grass. "Good thing I had my snake boots."

Betty gasped. "Why, what happened?"

With a flick of her hand, Flora waved off the question. "Stick that gas in the car. We're burning daylight."

Indeed, the sun would be setting soon. Betty emptied the gas can into Flora's SUV. They went back to the station for a full tank, then on the farm-to-market road toward the Smiths' house.

A dually truck pulling a trailer loaded with hay bales headed their way. Betty sucked in a breath.

"Don't you worry, none," Flora said. She slowed and pulled two wheels off the pavement, allowing plenty of room for the truck to pass.

Everybody in Tulip knew where the abandoned Sanchez place was. The clapboard house with its flaking, white paint and overgrown yard had been empty for a decade. A family was renting it when Betty first moved to Tulip in '93, but they moved to Odessa in 2010.

They passed several small ranches and crossed the creek over a concrete bridge not nearly as aesthetically pleasing nor historic as the covered bridge.

The house came into view just as the asphalt ended. Flora slowed her SUV on the dusty gravel road. With the sun dropping toward the horizon, the road took on an orange hue.

A window from the upstairs dormer faced the length of the road. Anyone standing there would have a good view of the road and surrounding landscape, but right now it was just an empty, rectangular hole.

"It looks like nobody's home." An unexplained chill crawled up Betty's spine. "Maybe they went to the lake for the weekend. It's certainly hot enough."

"Hotter than Hades, that's for sure. Now quit fussing. We're almost there."

The sky had darkened a shade. They should have called on the Smiths Sunday after church instead.

"Mr. Smith's Navigator isn't here," Flora said as they pulled into the drive. The roof sagged in a scowl. Gaps in the front porch balustrade left holes like missing teeth.

"How do you know what kind of car he drives?"

Flora unbuckled her seat belt. "Saw him and your Goth girl last month at the tire place on I-20. Even hermits need new tires now and then."

Betty climbed out of the car and shook her head. "His car would be worth more than this whole house. Why rent a shabby place if you could afford to buy something nicer? Anyway, I guess they're gone. We should leave."

Flora was already on the porch. The warped boards creaked under her weight.

A smell like dead varmints stung Betty's nose. The farmhouse had been empty for so long racoons or possums had apparently lived–and definitely died– under its floorboards and in its walls.

Flora knocked. "We can't just leave. The Navigator's gone, but Sylvia could still be here." The door swung halfway open.

Nobody was there.

Flora gasped. "It's a ghost," she whispered.

"Nonsense, the door wasn't latched is all." Betty joined her on the porch and called into the house. "Sylvia? Mr. Smith? It's Betty Bell."

No one answered.

Spinning about, Betty said, "We tried. Let's go." She headed down the porch steps but didn't hear Flora follow. Betty looked over her shoulder. The front door was wide open now, and Flora was nowhere to be seen.

Betty's heartbeat accelerated. "Flora!" She sprinted

up the stairs and into the house. From the entryway, there was a living room to the right, stairs to the left, and a narrow hallway straight ahead. If she looked beyond the living room, towards the back of the house, she could just make out a piece of the kitchen. Boxes stood in stacks near the living room fireplace. In the dim light they cast monstrous shadows on the wall.

"Flora?" Why was she whispering? Betty raised her voice. "Flora, where are you?" She hooked her purse over the stairway's newel post and tiptoed down the narrow hallway past cans of paint and rolls of wallpaper.

"It looks like they were fixing to spruce up the place," said Flora from behind.

Betty yelped and spun. "You startled me! Where were you?"

"I was in the kitchen and heard you calling." She was munching a saltine.

Eyeing the cracker, Betty said, "I thought you were on a grapefruit diet."

"I'm not too sure about the diet. Sounds like a fad to me."

They moved further down the hallway. A spider had strung a web in the corner of a doorway which led to a large bedroom.

Flora's phone chimed the hour, and both women jumped. The spider scurried to a far spoke of her web.

"Turn that thing off," Betty hissed.

"A little jumpy, eh? Could it be you're scared there's a haint 'round the corner?" Flora's eyebrows bounced as she grinned, but she silenced her phone.

Betty faced her friend. "I'm a little jumpy because we're trespassing." Truth was, she didn't feel good about the situation because black-clad, pale-skinned Sylvia didn't seem like a kid who'd want to go to the lake or out for pizza or anything typical like that.

Flora shrugged. "The door was ajar. We're just checking on the welfare of your student."

Suddenly, a child's giggle made them stiffen. It came from upstairs.

"Sylvia," cried Betty, "you're here! Are you okay? We're coming up." Betty brushed past her friend and took the stairs two at a time.

Flora plodded up behind her.

The two women ended up in a bedroom with exotic bird posters on the wall. Early evening sunlight poured through the mullioned dormer window and threw sharp X's on brilliant macaws, long-nosed toucans, and a kingfisher caught mid-splash with its prey. A small bookcase held classics and, to Betty's delight, dozens of her poetry books.

Flora pulled out one of Betty's books and flipped through it. "She was certainly a fan of yours. It looks like she has all sixty."

"Sixty-two. You always forget the two romance collections."

"It's more like romance has forgotten me."

"Maybe someday, Flora," Betty said as she read the spines of the non-Betty Bell books. *Frankenstein* by Mary Shelly. *The Dream Keeper* by Langston Hughes. Then *Shirley, Villette,* and *The Professor,* all Charlotte Bronte books.

"It's egg-frying hot up here," Flora said. "I'm going back downstairs."

"Right behind you." A well-loved paperback, *To Kill a Mockingbird,* sitting on the bed caught Betty's eye. "In a sec," she added. She thumbed through the book and through her memories. Books were a refuge in the dark years following her parents' accident. She stopped at a Polaroid picture that had been tucked between the pages. Taking the picture out for a closer look, she could see it was an image of a blonde girl, maybe twelve-to-fourteen, and an older boy with a sunburned nose who had his arm around her shoulders. They were standing in front of the East Weatherford High School gym. He smirked more than smiled, and his arm said *possessive* more than *caring*. "I don't like you," she said to his film-face.

A scream sounded from downstairs.

"Flora! I'm coming!" Betty dashed down the stairs.

"Jesus help us all!" Flora's voice was coming from the end of the narrow hallway. She always started her prayers at the women's circle by calling out to the Lord, but this didn't sound like any ordinary prayer.

"Jesus, oh, Jesus!"

Betty raced past the paint cans and wallpaper and ducked under the spider web. Flora had one hand over her mouth, her now-pale face peeking above her fingers, and the other hand pointed at the rubble on the floor.

Sylvia's legs, clad in black cargo pants, poked out from beneath the rubble. Flies and maggots swarmed the space between her sturdy boots and the hem of her pants. She was very much dead.

Chapter 5

*She exists in the nothing life
between the folds of humanity's skin.*

At once, Betty realized the "dead raccoon" smell she had noticed earlier was a dead *human.* She crossed herself though she wasn't Catholic. It was a habit she had picked from attending mass with her second set of fosters.

Betty placed a hand on her best friend's shoulder. Flora turned, and the two women embraced. Flora trembled at first then relaxed.

After a moment, they released one another. Flora had calmed down enough to whip out her phone and turn it on.

"Thanks for calling 911, Flora," Betty said. A wave of sadness threatened to double her over. "May she rest in peace."

"Do you think her grandfather did it?" Flora's voice was tight, shaky.

"Flora, no!"

"Where is he, then? If he didn't kill her, then who did?" Flora held up her phone and turned in a circle.

"Sylvia, it's me, Miss Williams, and Mrs. Bell, too. Who killed you?"

"Knock it off." Betty smacked at the phone in Flora's hand. "It was an accident. A house this old, things falling down around them..."

"Then where's Mr. Smith?"

Betty had no answer for that. "Fine. I'll call Miller directly." Ever since LB had returned to Tulip after college graduation, he and the slightly older Deputy Miller, who went by plain old *Miller,* had become fast friends. Betty had Miller on speed dial. She retreated to the stairway and dug her phone out of her purse.

With orders from Miller to not touch anything and to "exit the house *immediately*," Betty and Flora waited in the SUV with the air running.

Betty turned the Polaroid around and around in her hand. She hadn't realized she was still holding onto it when they went outside.

Miller's patrol car pulled into the drive ten minutes later–Betty recognized the dent over the left front fender–followed shortly by another deputy. The two men went to work inside doing whatever gruesome things law enforcement people did around dead bodies. Images from television mystery series flashed in Betty's brain. She tossed them away with a shake of her head. "I'll be right back, Flora. I need to give this photo to Miller."

"You can't," she said, grabbing Betty's arm. "It's got your fingerprints all over it."

Betty pulled her arm away. "I keep telling you, we don't know that the girl was murdered. She probably died in an accident."

"And I keep telling you it's suspicious that her

grandfather is missing."

Betty caught a glimpse of the western sky in the side mirror. The sun had dipped below the horizon. "It's getting late. I'm going to give Miller the photo and ask again if we can leave."

Flora shrugged. "Suit yourself. I'll come visit you behind bars."

Betty approached the porch stairs just as Miller was coming down. "Stop right there," he said.

"I just wanted to give you this picture. I found it upstairs."

"Oh fer crying out–what were you doing upstairs?"

"Making sure Sylvia was okay." She closed her hands over the photo, wanting to hold onto it for a little while longer. It wasn't a picture of Sylvia, but it was obviously people important to her, and in that way, it was a connection to the girl.

Miller held out an evidence bag. "Drop it in here."

"It was an accident, right?" She dropped the photo into the bag. "The old ceiling fell."

Miller grimaced. "Did you touch the sledgehammer?"

"What sledgehammer? Someone used a *sledgehammer* on her? You mean it wasn't an accident?" Betty curled over in horror.

With a hand patting Betty's back, Miller said, "I was just coming out to talk to you." His voice was gentle. "The coroner is on her way. As soon as I get some info from you and Flora, you all can go."

After Miller questioned the women separately, they left.

"See?" Flora said. They were nearing Highway 6. "Sylvia lashed out at her grandfather while he was demolishing a wall, and it got out of hand, and he already had the sledgehammer in his hand, and..."

Betty stopped listening. She remembered Sylvia's poem about the blissful drive through the country. She pictured the girl's bedroom with its beautiful bird posters and a bookshelf of classics. It was hard to imagine Sylvia, despite her darkly assertive clothing and Betty's first impression of the girl, lashing out. Could she have gotten in a physical altercation with her grandfather? She was calm in class, lethargic, even. Betty wished she knew the girl better.

Pulling her phone out, Betty said, "I should text LB the awful news. He'll wonder why I've been gone so long."

"Miller told us not to talk about it."

"I know, but LB can keep his mouth shut. Besides, if I try to hide something from him, he can always tell."

"Yeah," Flora said, "your eye twitches."

They turned onto the highway.

There was a text from Flora waiting on Betty's phone. It was an image of the photo Betty had just turned over to Miller. Tears flooded her eyes. She tried to thank Flora, but a sob came out of her mouth instead.

Flora patted Betty's leg. "I know, hon, I know."

After a while, Betty's tears faded, and the two women drove in silence.

A wild boar trotted across the road in front of Flora's headlights. "Watch out for the pig. How fast are you going? Shouldn't you have your high beams on?"

In the morning, Betty scanned *The Tulip Times* Sunday edition while LB made coffee. "I don't see anything about the murder," she said. She returned to page one and flipped through the paper again.

LB placed a Corelle cup full of steamy, dark goodness in front of Betty, then said, "Miller probably wants to notify the next of kin before he talks to a journalist. Did you know women journalists in the US outnumber men journalists fifty-three to forty-seven?" He took a sip of his own coffee then kissed her. His lips were warm and moist.

Betty divided the paper, the front half with the headlines and the puzzle page for LB, and the back half with the local news and the sports for herself.

"But how's Miller going to notify Sylvia's next of kin?" Betty asked. "She lived with her grandfather, and he is nowhere to be found."

"He's missing because he's the killer. He fled town."

With a huff, Betty said, "No, not her grandfather. You know I have a knack for spotting endangered kids." She had seen too many when she was in the System. "Sylvia was a loner not because she was abused but because…" She couldn't put her finger on it, but there was something about Sylvia's situation that was other than a kid in a bad home.

She retrieved Sylvia's notebook that the girl had left behind in class. "I feel like I'm spying on her, but I guess it doesn't matter if she's passed on." Betty tapped the notebook. "Maybe there's information in here about Sylvia or her grandfather that Miller could use."

"Isn't that Miller's call, not yours?" LB folded his half of the paper to a neat little rectangle with the crossword on top then clicked his pen.

Avoiding LB's gaze, Betty shrugged. "Maybe. I'll just take a peek, you know, in case it'd be a big waste of Miller's time."

LB grunted but continued on with his crossword.

Flipping through the notebook, Betty found short diary entries, doodles of birds, a half page of notes on Japanese syllabic poetry–she was definitely paying attention that day in class–and quite a few poems.

There was always something left of the artist–any kind of artist be it sculptor, painter, or poet–in his or her work. Betty stopped on one of the poems.

"LB, listen to this. Sylvia wrote a paragraph describing her grandfather's morning routine with his medicines and getting cleaned up and such. It's followed by this poem."

> *The years a pending pall,*
> *His quaking hand around a cup.*
> *I catch his fork ere it falls.*
> *Coffee drips, I loathe disrupt*
> *Our blessed breakfast chat.*

In the margin next to the poem there was a smiley face and a note that said, *I'll wash the tablecloth later.*

Betty adjusted the notebook to cover her own coffee drips she had left on the newspaper.

"What teenager uses words like *quaking* and *loathe*?" LB asked.

"Never mind that. I knew she was more mature, more advanced than the other kids, but I am surprised the word *blessed* was even in the girl's vocabulary. You should have seen her. Black clothes, clodhoppers, tattoos." Betty drew her hand slowly across the notebook page, thinking. "Then again, I didn't get a chance to really know her." The indents from Sylvia's big, block letters were braille to Betty's fingertips.

Betty didn't know braille. But she did know poetry. With a little effort, she was sure she could come to understand Sylvia through her writings.

Crossing off another crossword clue, LB asked, "What's your point?"

"My point is this is a poem from a girl who loved her grandfather. She practically sponge-bathed him, his back, anyway." She read from another poem.

> *He sits shirtless, ashamed.*
> *A soapy rag I draw across his pale back.*
> *Moles and veins.*

"Apparently," Betty said, "he couldn't reach his back. She tied his shoes, too. He needed her. I can't see her turning on him, and I can't see him attacking her."

"Maybe." He filled in another word of the puzzle and checked off the clue.

Betty turned the page. "Oh, look at this." Her voice grew thick. "She was looking forward to turning eighteen on July third. She died just before her birthday."

LB looked up from his crossword. "Eighteen, so young. This murder business is no good."

They sat in silence for a moment, then LB said, "Did you know more people have their birthdays in August than any other month?"

"Why in the world did Mr. Smith flee? If I drove, I'd go all over the county looking for him myself. Of course, I don't think the Lord made our bodies to go that fast."

LB harrumphed. "And I don't think the good Lord has anything to do with it, because God hasn't given us the spirit of fear," he said, paraphrasing a verse in the Bible. "You're the one keeping yourself from driving. Just think, you let me drive you around."

"For short distances." She glared at him. What was he getting at?

"You let Flora drive you around."

"While hanging on for dear life." She pushed away from the table and went to the sink to start dishes. Loudly. And scrubbing with vigor.

After a minute, he came up behind her and placed his arms gently around her waist. His breath was on her neck. It felt like a warm caress.

Dang it, he had a way of quelling her temper even when she didn't want it quelled.

"You'll drive when you find a good reason to let go of your fear." He moved next to her and started rinsing the dishes. "At any rate," he said after a while, "*The Tulip Times* has nothing about the murder, at least not today, and we need to get to church."

The next day, Betty was at the kitchen table reading more of Sylvia's notebook when LB's muffled voice crept out of the master bedroom. He was probably on a business call.

A moment later, LB came into the kitchen and refilled his coffee cup. "Mr. Smith's car was abandoned on I-20."

"Was that Miller? Mr. Smith's car broke down? Did he say who killed his precious granddaughter?" Betty gripped the notebook so hard the spiral binding bit into her palm. "Did Miller arrest the killer?"

"You're calling Sylvia Smith *precious* now? You only knew her for a short time, and you were positively frightened of her at first."

"Yeah, because on the first day of class she wrote a disturbing poem full of violence and cussing and all sorts of horrible things. I think she was testing me. Besides, it was a very good poem, just not appropriate for a class full of teenagers." Betty tapped the notebook. "I'm getting to know her even better now. I'm learning a lot about all the kids through their poetry. Take Julie, for example, Mercurial swings of emotions. Hank, nature-inspired. Juan, all sing-song and rhymes, rather upbeat that young man. Bridget–"

Putting his hands up in a *stop* motion, LB said, "Okay, I get it, I get it." He sat down at the table next to her, his jaw set.

Betty knew that look. He had something to say that would disappoint her.

Just then her stomach cramped and let out a rumble loud enough to make the walls of Jericho fall.

LB slouched back in his chair and laughed. "I told you not to eat Elrod's grits at the covered dish supper last night," he said, putting *grits* in air quotes. "He doesn't like to waste *any* part of a deer he tags."

"Ew." She rubbed her tummy and told it to calm down. "Now tell me what you didn't want to tell me.

LB's expression turned serious. Leaning forward, he took one of Betty's hands in both of his. "The keys were in Mr. Smith's car, and it started perfectly, had plenty of gas, too. Miller said the old man played one over on everybody. He got away clean as a whistle."

She pulled her hand back. "Miller shouldn't be sharing his work with you."

LB shrugged. "You know how he is."

"Did he say anything about any other relatives, her parents maybe?"

"No, but something must have happened to them if she was living with her grandfather." He downed his coffee, rose, and kissed Betty on the top of her head before heading back to his office.

Betty gazed out the back window. A solitary finch flitted across the back yard then disappeared in the branches of the pecan tree. The refrigerator droned. Her stomach cramped again, but this time it was because she was convinced Miller was after the wrong suspect.

Betty snapped up her phone and called him. "I have Sylvia Smith's class notebook."

"Does it have anything to do with the murder? A motive or names and dates?" A horn honked in the background. He was driving.

He knows better than to talk and drive at the same time. She needed to hurry and spit it out before he got in a wreck. "Not exactly, but she wrote down feelings and class assignments, a breakfast poem, and–"

"Sounds about as useful as tits on a bull. Gotta go." He hung up.

Betty resisted the urge to throw her phone. She set it down carefully before flipping through more pages of Sylvia's notebook. She stopped at a haiku.

soft shades of silence

WHEN DID WE LOSE SYLVIA?

we huddled in the old house
evil lurks outdoors

"That girl was scared of something, and it wasn't her grandfather."

Tuesday morning Betty skipped breakfast and went straight to her office in her pajamas. She needed to come up with some Plains-inspired poems for her next collection. *Of Dust and Daisies: Poetry from the Northern Plains of Texas* would be the followup to *Of Canyons and Kayaks: Poetry from the Pecos River*.

As she often did when facing a blank page but not having any ideas, Betty started with a central subject, the live oak in this case.

Live oaks were plentiful in the Plains. They were fire resistant, drought resistant, and tough as stewed skunk. (Which she had eaten thanks to another one of Elrod's covered dish contributions.) But Tulip's live oaks didn't resemble the trees she remembered from her childhood in Waco. Tulip's live oaks were short and leaned to one side as if the wind had sculpted the mighty oak into a bonsai.

She wrote "live oak" in the middle of a fresh page in her notebook then drew a circle around it.

From somewhere in the house, LB's laugh broke the silence.

She drew lines leading away from the circle like the spokes of a bicycle wheel. At the end of each spoke, she wrote down whatever words came to mind when thinking about pin oaks.

Quickly, quickly, quickly, don't stop to judge, she remembered her college professor saying when he taught the technique.

Tree, rugged, tough, gnarled, bonsai, pin oak, post oak, mesquite, she wrote.

LB's laughter morphed into a cough. He must have laughed too hard.

Hornets, poor soil, wind.

She stopped there and picked one of the words, *mesquite,* as a new hub and repeated the process.

Spine, thorns, buffalo, Texas, stickers, heat, desert.

LB broke into a new round of laughter with deep, guttural guffaws.

She picked one of the words, *thorns*, and repeated the process yet again.

Her college professor had explained this method of diagramming free associations was called *mind-mapping.* Betty thought it looked like a snowflake rather than a map, but whatever.

Crown of thorns, lion, sand, Jesus.

LB took a loud, wheezing breath and started laughing again. Betty slapped her pen down and went to see what all the fuss was about.

He was at the kitchen table, *The Tulip Times* spread before him. His face was scarlet, and tears ran down his cheeks.

She put her hands on her hips. "Control yourself, LB, you're going to have a heart attack."

"Betty!" He jabbed his finger at the headline of an article in the local section, and Betty leaned over his shoulder to read it.

MAYOR HIRES CHICKEN AS NEW BODYGUARD

The mayor of Tulip, Buford Helper, bought Roberta from Elrod Snew Cooter, local chicken farmer and certified dog surfing instructor. Roberta is a gray-feathered, Aseel-hybrid chicken. In speaking to citizens at the latest town hall meeting, Mayor Helper explained, "People say Elrod's got the meanest chickens in the county. I believe it's true." He held up his right hand to show the small crowd. Half his pinky finger was missing. "Then the idea hit me," Helper continued. "If I hire a chicken for a bodyguard to replace my former bodyguard–Kenneth dyed his hair blue and moved to Key West–then I can save the City of Tulip a chunk of money. We pay Roberta in meal worms and grubs. Why, with just the savings in payroll taxes, we can upgrade the science lab at the high school."

When *The Tulip Times* approached Mr. Cooter for a quote, he said, "The dog surfing business in this part of Texas has been slow."

Betty swatted LB upside the head then went back to her office.

Chapter 6
other people's words
like secret whispered wisdom
or lies screamed on high

That Saturday at the beginning of class, Betty wrote "Blackout Poetry" on the classroom chalkboard in large, cursive letters. She quickly erased it and reminded herself to print.

It'd been a week since Betty and Flora discovered Sylvia's body. Betty had been collecting and re-reading the newspaper at night, scouring every section for some mention of the crime. With her stack of accumulated newspapers, she felt now was as good a time as any to introduce the kids to blackout poetry, and what better medium than the local newspaper which, apparently, they had no experience reading because, as Bridget had explained the first day of class, newspapers are "for old people."

Betty handed out sections of newspaper, careful not to give sports to Juan, community happenings to Julie, or politics to Darlene. She wanted to stretch the kids beyond their typical interests.

"What's blackout poetry?" Bridget asked.

"You're giving Juan politics? I wanted politics. Can I have his?" Darlene said.

"Politics, cool." Juan pointed to the headlines. "Voters vent heated concerns over inflation. Global temperatures rise." The class cracked up, Bridget whooped, and Hank gave Juan a high-five.

Betty snatched the paper out of Juan's hands. "That is not what it says!" She gave him the obituaries instead.

"Then can I have politics?" Darlene said. Her voice had turned whiny, and an ache took hold of the muscles in Betty's neck.

Odessa Lynn whispered something to Julie.

"The old, gross Sanchez house?" Julie said. "Ew, I'm getting black stuff on my hands."

Jorge wadded up one of his pages and launched it high in the air. It landed with a crinkling sound in the trash can. Other students quickly followed suit, throwing balls of paper at the trash can and at each other like a midsummer snowball fight.

Betty tore up the remaining newspapers then slammed the shredded pile in the wastebasket. The class went silent. They stared.

She felt her cheeks warm. Should she continue with the newspaper poetry? Julie wiped her hands on Odessa Lynn's shirt. Odessa Lynn's jaw tensed, but she said nothing. Betty could change the lesson, but she'd have to wing it because she had nothing else planned.

A series of taps at the windows drew Betty's attention. More than two dozen grasshoppers clung to the glass, and she was reminded that she had made it through that first, horrible class. Meanwhile, Julie examined her fingertips. Santiago held a wadded ball of paper in his hands and was eyeing the trash can.

She shook her head at him, and he laid the paper ball on his desk. For now.

I only have them one day a week. How do parents deal with this every day?

She decided to carry on with the blackout poetry lesson. "Let me read you a short poem." Betty opened her folder, not letting the students see the paper from which she was reading.

> *Thirsty fields fading*
> *Crumbled earth in hand*
> *Relentless*
> *He sought*
> *life*

Hank frowned. "That doesn't sound like one of your poems, Mrs. Bell."

"But it does sound like Papa dealing with the drought," said Santiago in perfect English. Jorge and the twins' parents owned a small ranch.

Betty raised an eyebrow at Santiago, his twin, and their older brother. "Don't you think it's high time you three cut the English-Spanish charade?"

Jorge bit his lower lip and looked at Betty.

"You're welcome to stay, Jorge."

He gave her such a big smile that she forgave him for starting the snowball fight earlier. And both of you," she said, nodding at Hank then Santiago, "are correct about my poem."

She flipped the folder around and showed the kids an article from the paper. Using a felt pen, she had marked out all but eleven words. "The eleven words that I haven't marked out create my poem."

The grasshoppers had vanished. Betty was on her own, and it was okay. "It doesn't sound like my normal poems, Hank, because I was working with someone else's words. And it does sound like the drought, Santiago, because this is an article from the weather section of the newspaper. This style of poetry is called 'blackout poetry.'"

Julie squealed. "I get it!" She flattened her part of the newspaper and started scribbling out words.

"Me, too," the normally quiet Odessa Lynn said. She pulled a marker out of her backpack and flipped her braids over her shoulder before boldly wiping out entire lines of text.

Odessa Lynn was a base on the cheerleading squad or sometimes a back spot. She was one of the squad members who had the mass and strength to toss smaller cheerleaders into the air or, when she was playing the role of a back spot, stabilize them once they were up there and catch their heads and shoulders on the way down. Betty smiled when she realized how ignorant she'd been about cheerleading terms when she first moved to Tulip. For at least a decade now, no one had said to her, *You ain't from around here, are you?*

Betty gave the kids fifteen minutes to work on their blackout poems.

When the allotted time had passed, students were eager to read their poems. Betty was pleased they understood the assignment. Sebastian delivered his poem accompanied by a look of worry on his face.

Divining rods wobble and sway,

No water is found, not today.

"It's an article about drilling for well water," he said.

Odessa Lynn's poem was like a thought caught in midair. Darlene's poem "frolicked, skipped, hopped, and cavorted" across the page. "It was an article about white tail deer mating season," she said.

Bridget raised her hand. "Mizz Bell, can I go next?"

Julie huffed. "What do you mean *Mizz* Bell? When did you become such a country girl?"

Betty was about to point out that everyone living in the tiny, rural town of Tulip could be classified as country, but Jorge beat her to it, in a manner of speaking.

"Cities suck," he said.

Julie's nostrils flared. "Well Hank and I can't wait to leave this stupid little town and move to a big city. Dallas, Austin, anywhere but here. Right, Hunk?"

Hank didn't seem to hear. His gaze was fixed somewhere out the window.

"Right," Julie declared for him.

Betty raised her voice. "Let's get back to the task at hand. Bridget, please read your poem."

Bridget had the local section with an article about an older woman who'd suffered a heart attack and Cletus who was her heroic nurse. Bridget had drawn a large cross in blue ballpoint pen and colored in all of the cross except three words:

My
Heart

Rescued

"That's good, Bridget," Juan said in an usually serious (for him) voice. "Really good." He tilted his head to the side and smiled at her.

Betty felt her eyes begin to water. "Powerful, Bridget," was all she could manage. She swallowed. "And we still have Hank's poem, if you'd like to share."

He nodded.

a Lady and a Bird
orchids
poppies
traffic beautified

"Orchids and poppies? Ew, Hank!" Julie crossed her arms over her chest. "You wrote a poem about flowers."

Color crawled up Hank's neck, and Betty rushed to rescue him. She held up his part of the paper. "He got the history section, an article about Lady Bird Johnson's work to beautify our country's highways."

Julie rolled her eyes. "Whoever *that* is."

Hank yanked the paper from Betty's hand and jammed it in his backpack. "I'm out of here."

Betty and Julie spoke at the same time. "There's no need to leave" and "If you walk out, I'm not giving you a ride home."

Juan and Bridget exchanged looks, both with pursed O-lips and wide eyes.

A cruel smile spread across Odessa Lynn's face, and Betty wondered if there was a love triangle going on. She positioned herself so Julie wouldn't have to see the other girl's expression.

"Well," Betty said, "it's almost time for class to be dismissed anyway, so–"

Chair legs screeched on the floor. A cuss word flew from Darlene's mouth in her exuberant exchange with Bridget. Students left in pairs and trios.

"Wait, Darlene," Julie said, "I'll drive you home." But Darlene either didn't hear Julie or ignored her.

Julie shuffled out alone.

What did that girl have against flowers?

After church the next day, Betty went through *The Tulip Times* and looked for any hint of the crime or even a line about Mr. Smith's abandoned car and his disappearance. Nothing. Nor was there anything about the murder in Monday's paper. By Tuesday, Betty was fuming.

"I'm going to call the paper, LB, and I'm going to find out what's going on."

"What's a five-letter word for *intrepidity*?" he said.

"Intre-what? I can't even say it."

He winked at her. "Moxie. You've got moxie, Betty. Just be careful not to jeopardize Miller's investigation."

Betty went to her desk in the office to grab her phone. Just as she got there, her phone pinged with a notification. She had forgotten her Zoom meeting with Adhira, her agent in Dallas. Betty sat down in front of her laptop and brought up the Zoom app.

"Hi, Adhira," Betty managed with a smile. She wondered if she had scrambled eggs in her teeth and peered at her video image next to Adhira's on the screen.

She also worried about the state of her office on camera. An office-plus: Plus a broken side table standing at an odd angle (part of LB's honey-do list). Plus folded tee shirts on the canister vacuum cleaner which somehow only vacuumed half the room yesterday. Plus a book bag hanging from the arm of her desk chair.

Morning sun turned fingerprints on the window to luminescent streaks. Betty pushed the laptop to the corner of her desk, angling its camera away from the window.

Now her camera saw empty coffee cups and a bowl of half-eaten peanuts. There was a large mason jar, empty and washed, eager for its next job. A box of tissues awaited her next allergy-laden day.

Poetry books lay everywhere, hers and others'.

Near her foot, a desiccated spider lay on its back. She flicked it away even though she knew Adhira couldn't see it.

Betty squirmed. An odor like cow patties marinating in balsamic vinegar burst from her armpits. How did Adhira do that to her?

"*Of Dust and Daisies*, Betty, talk to me," Adhira said.

Betty hesitated a second too long.

"Betty, no. Don't tell me you're behind. What do you need to get going on this collection, chocolate, coffee, a massage? Put LB on the phone, and we'll work up some kind of writing retreat." The woman talked twice as fast as a normal human being, and Betty had to concentrate to keep up. "Have you ever been to Brekenridge, Betty? It's not too far from you."

"No, I–"

"Me, either, but people tell me the B-and-Bs there are good, especially near the lake. Nice, quiet place to get some writing done."

Betty was shaking her head.

"Not a writing retreat? Then what do you want?"

I want Sylvia's killer caught. I want the newspaper to say something about the poor girl or at least her missing grandfather. "Nothing, Adhira. I'll get to work." She mustered a smile. "Promise."

"Good, then let's look at your marketing plan. The publisher set you up for a presentation in Amarillo, but I know how you don't like road trips, so I nixed that." Adhira listed three libraries and a senior center.

Betty's head felt like it was floating. Didn't Adhira ever take a breath? *Maybe it's me who needs to take a breath.* Betty heaved in a big lungful of air.

"You look like you're going to faint, Betty. Are you going to faint?"

"No, I–"

"Don't look like you're going to faint when you're giving your presentations, or they'll never ask you back. I also nixed the junior high school talk in Mineral Wells because we know how you are with children, especially after the nursery catastrophe at the church."

How did she hear about that? "I wouldn't go so far as to call it a catastrophe."

"Stay on point, Betty. Time is money. I've got ideas for in-person book signings in Eastland and Cisco, four book club Zoom presentations, and a seminar at Ranger College. Let's work on the plan of attack so we don't duplicate the publisher's efforts, and we need to block out your schedule."

Then they talked about the publisher's needs. "Don't stray too far from the first book, Betty, style-wise I mean. The publisher is expecting a similar book, a sister-book to *Canyons*."

By the time they said goodbye, Betty's hand was cramping (from taking so many notes), her bladder was full, and she had a headache brewing.

Brewing. Betty needed another cup of hot, aromatic coffee. After one stop at the bathroom and another stop at the coffee pot, Betty finally had a moment to call *The Tulip Times*.

"I'd like to speak to the editor, please."

Sounds of chewing came through the phone.

With a glance at the microwave clock, Betty noted it was almost noon.

"Me," said the lunchtime chewer.

"Why haven't you published anything about the mur–" Betty caught herself. If Miller hadn't talked to a reporter yet, maybe she'd hamper his investigation by alerting the killer through a newspaper article that Sylvia's body had been found. Or something. She wasn't actually sure how the mind of a killer worked.

But maybe she could help Miller find Mr. Smith if everyone knew he was missing. Someone might have seen him.

Betty tried again. "Why haven't you published anything about the man and his granddaughter who went missing last week or maybe it was the week before?"

A slurp. "Yeah? Where's this?"

"The old Sanchez place."

He smacked his lips. He was certainly a loud eater. "Is that even in Tulip? I think it's outside town. Besides, nobody lives in that old place. Ought to be torn down. Anyway, I haven't heard anything."

"Sylvia Smith and her grandfather recently moved in. Now they're missing."

"Never heard of 'em."

Outside the kitchen window, a mockingbird sought shelter in the only shade left, beneath the house's eave. The bird settled on the windowsill and watched Betty. *Sylvia would have liked that a bird was interested in her case.*

"Nobody's going to want to read about these Snydor people," the man continued.

"Smith, their last name is Smith."

"Whatever. They're nobodies. Call me back when you get real news, 'kay?"

"But–"

He hung up.

She took a swig of coffee. Her hands shook in anger, and a bit of the aromatic drink dribbled over the edge of her cup. The morning's newspaper was still spread out on the kitchen table. (LB liked to say they enjoyed *lingering* over the paper.) She turned to the masthead and plunked her wet cup on the editor's face.

The Smiths were *not* nobodies. And now Mr. Smith was who-knows-where and probably in fear. Otherwise, why did he leave? He was alone, grieving. A sharp pain pricked at Betty's heart. It was the same pain she had felt when her parents died. Betty was fifteen at the time. Well-meaning adults, most of them strangers, said all the wrong things.

You're young. Young people get over things quickly.

Kids are resilient.

You'll make friends at your new school. But smile, or they won't want to make friends with a Sad Sally.

Sylvia had been a brilliant teen, much smarter than Betty was at that age. "Oh, Sylvia," Betty said quietly. "A creative soul, a talented poet, fearfully and wonderfully made. It's like the killer, the editor, and everyone else is content with erasing your memory from the face of the earth."

Anger rose, flooding Betty's senses. She slapped the kitchen table. No one was going to erase a child of God on Betty's watch. "Besides, I'm too old to *get over things quickly.*" Since *The Tulip Times* was unhelpful, she decided to see what she could find online about the Smiths and about the two teens in the photograph. Maybe she'd find something that would help Miller's case along. She fetched her laptop.

It was almost dinner when LB emerged from the master bedroom.

"'Bout time you took a break," Betty said. "You've been working straight all afternoon." She was still at the kitchen table, making good use of Mr. Google.

Peering at her screen, he asked, "What are you researching, Halloween costumes?" He pecked her on the cheek.

"The Smiths." She laughed despite herself. It was foolish to have thought she'd get anywhere with searches like "teen couple at East Weatherford High." There were 503,000 results, none of the first 600 she looked at were the mystery couple. She tried "Sylvia Smith Weatherford." Over two million results, and the closest "Sylvia" image that matched her late student was a sixty-two-year-old exotic dancer with an Elvira wig. (Thus LB's question about Halloween.) Earlier, Betty had tried "Sylvia Smith birds," expecting Sylvia to have a Pinterest board of pied crows or an Instagram account with indigo buntings. Or *some*thing. But no luck.

"It's odd, LB. What kid nowadays doesn't even have a social media account?"

As soon as The Tulip Grocer opened Wednesday, Betty laced up her sneakers and hurried over. *My hunt for Mr. Smith has begun!*

She pushed her shopping buggy down the coffee aisle, the most natural choice for a false shopping trip. She tossed four bags of coffee into her buggy but couldn't think of what else to get. There was a person banging on the store's front windows. Probably a window cleaner. Betty ignored the ruckus and took her buggy to Jacqueline's checkout stand.

Eyes that blinked too fast greeted Betty. Jacqueline's cheeks were ruddy, not with rouge but heat that radiated through a layer of makeup.

"Jacqueline, are you okay?"

The cashier flashed her bright teeth. "A little suffering today is nothing compared… to… glory be.

Or however it goes." She looked down and swiped the first bag of coffee. A clump of her too big hair fell over her forehead. Betty's gaze followed the cashier's hand as she pushed it back into place.

There was a line, a scrape from Jacqueline's eyebrow across her forehead–where wrinkles that once existed had been smoothed over by a physician's needle–and into her hairline. "Did you hurt yourself?"

The banging at the window sped up. Betty finally turned and saw Flora mouthing something from the other side of the glass. Her colorful figure made a marching motion then a driving motion. Betty shrugged, unable to process her friend's wild articulations, and turned back toward the issue at hand.

"I was wondering," said Betty in as casual a voice as she could manage given the circumstances, and without saying anything to get on Miller's bad side, "if you've seen Mr. Smith around?" Betty certainly hadn't told anyone, save LB, that Sylvia was dead. Surely Flora hadn't, either. "Or Sylvia, of course. Sylvia, too."

Jacqueline stopped mid-swipe of the second bag. It was vanilla coffee.

I picked up vanilla? I don't like vanilla flavored coffee.

"Um." Jacqueline's gaze scanned the ceiling.

The scrape on Jacqueline's face. Her distress over Sylvia's arrival in Tulip. A dark thought passed through Betty's mind, and she pushed it aside.

"Did you?" Betty said. "See the Smiths, I mean?"

Flora poked her head in the front door. "Psst! Betty."

Betty waved her away and turned her attention back to Jacqueline.

She swiped the final bag–another vanilla–and rang up the total. "Maybe we should get some more goats. Julie is fiercely protective of the goats." She leaned in and reached for Betty's hand.

Betty pulled her hands out of reach remembering the last time she and Jacqueline held hands.

In a whisper, Jacqueline said, "I need to tell you about–"

"Mrs. Ivy," said a diminutive man approaching the checkout stand. It was Mr. Stevens, the owner of The Tulip Grocer and Jacqueline's boss. "Diaz is out sick. Can you make the Fort Worth payroll run for me?"

"Sure," she said, all white smile and bright eyes. Her normal color returned. Looking at Betty, she said, "Fernando always makes the payroll run, but he's been out sick two days. Oh!" She pressed her hands on either side of her face. "I forgot to add him to my prayer list. No wonder he's still sick."

"Jacqueline, I don't think that's how prayer–" Betty stopped herself. Jacqueline had snapped out of whatever fog she was in, and Betty didn't want to rock the boat.

"And don't you worry. I'm praying for you to be a better teacher."

Betty mumbled her thanks around clenched teeth. She took the floppy plastic grocery bag–*really, I should use cloth bags more often*–and headed outside.

"Finally!" In her excitement, Flora practically chest bumped Betty.

"Why aren't you at work?" Betty aimed toward home via her walking route, but Flora steered her toward the Blazer.

"That's what I've been trying to tell you. A pipe

broke in the office. I have the day off while the plumbers are in the building. I can drive you to Weatherford."

"Why would I want to go to Weatherford?" The sun's heat radiated off the blacktop. She was afraid to stand still for fear of melting the soles of her shoes.

"The picture. Don't you get it? We can look for the blonde girl and the boy."

Things were getting clear. The driving motion Flora was doing at the window. "Why were you marching?"

Flora dropped her arms at her sides and threw her head back as if asking the Lord Himself to knock some sense into Betty. "Everybody knows East Weatherford won this year's state marching band competition."

"I see." Betty stepped a little to the side so she'd be standing mostly on paint delineating a parking space. It was cooler than plain asphalt. "Thanks anyway, Flora, but we can't just wander the streets of a city with a population of 33,000 and expect to run into a nameless girl and boy from a photograph. Besides, the photo was worn. We don't know how long ago it was taken and how the kids look today."

Flora shrugged. "I'll drive you home, then."

They opened the SUV's doors wide and let the superheated air escape before climbing in.

Flora started the car and danced her fingertips along the steering wheel. "Too hot. I can't hold it yet." She aimed the air conditioner vent at the steering wheel. "By the way, I told Lily Grace Holiday you'd help her with Elrod's chickens while he's down in Galveston working on his dog surfing instructor recertification."

"He's actually getting recertified? Tulip is 400

miles from the coast. This is the land of mesquite, cows, and pin oak." Flora's words dawned on Betty. "Wait, you *what?* Flora, I don't know anything about chickens." She cringed when she thought of Mayor Helper's missing pinky finger. "Are you sure it's safe? It's Homer's little brother. Why can't Homer go?"

Flora patted the steering wheel then gripped it. She put the car in gear. "Because Homer's on a fishing trip, and before you ask, the Holiday boys, including Mr. Holiday, went with him. Mrs. Holiday can't help because she hasn't recovered from her fall out of the pecan tree, bless her heart."

Narrowing her eyes at Flora, Betty asked, "And why can't *you* help Lily Grace?"

A moan escaped Flora's lips. "She's dumb as all get out. All the Holiday kids are. I had to suffer through all four stair-step children when I taught junior high Sunday school while you were busy creating an apocalyptic disaster in the church nursery."

Betty winced. Wasn't anybody going to let her forget about the church nursery? Pastor Bethany had finally suggested Betty teach the Savvy Silver Seniors class instead.

Flora turned onto Betty's road.

"It's not nice of you to say that about the Holiday kids," Betty said. "Besides, there's a difference between stupid and ignorant."

"Tomato, Tah-mah-to," Flora said, pulling into Betty's drive. "Lily Grace only needs help for one morning. Elrod will be back in town by supper." Flora put the car in park but left it running with the A/C on full blast. "Meet her at Elrod's gate tomorrow, sunrise."

"You told her I'd be there at sunrise?" *And why is*

Flora my best friend?

"So, seven-thirty or eight in the morning?"

"It's July. Try six o'clock. *I'm* not getting up that early."

Flora dropped her gaze and picked at the lint on her skirt. "Please don't make me go, Betty. The poor girl deserves someone who's nice to her, and all I did was yell at her every Sunday for two years straight when she was a thick-skulled pubescent. Now that she broke up with Fernando, the poor thing's probably a mess and could use some mama-ing."

Playing the mother card, that's a low blow, Flora. "You had no right to… Hold on, you mean she's been dating Fernando?"

Flora nodded.

Maybe Lily Grace could tell Betty why Fernando was so upset on the phone. He certainly had a temper. Was he violent? Did he know Sylvia?

"I'll do it," Betty said. Surely a few little hens wouldn't be that dangerous if she was mindful of her fingers.

Flora seemed lost in thought.

"I said I'd do it, Flora. What's wrong?"

She smiled. "Oh, nothing. I was just thinking about Mrs. Holiday. She makes the best pecan pie."

On that they could agree.

"Thanks for agreeing to help Lily Grace, Betty. Unless Loopy Brain wants to drive you, I'll pick you up just before six tomorrow morning. That way you don't have to walk over there in the dark."

The next morning, Flora dropped Betty off at Elrod's gate. The chirrups of the crickets were winding down, and the sky to the east was a peachy glow. Lily Grace unlocked the pipe fence gate and held it open for Betty.

There were nails piled up at the edge of the entrance. "What's with all the nails, Lily Grace?"

"Elrod scattered nails to stop chicken thieves from getting very far." Her west Texas accent was so thick you could hack it with an ax, and Betty suspected Lily Grace's manner of speaking had to do with the Holiday family's long history in Tulip. Same with Miller, the Cooter family, and Cletus. Cletus was Tulip's only Uber driver (as well as the heroic nurse from the blackout poetry lesson).

"Trouble was," Lily Grace continued, "he gave hisself a lot of flat tires. He said he didn't mind none. He likes shooting the breeze while Petrol Pete fixes flats. But it got expensive after a time, so he raked the nails to the side and got hisself Aseels."

Betty assumed Aseels were some sort of security device. "Did you know Pete isn't the gas station owner's real name?"

"Yes, ma'am. Word has it that he bought the gas station from the man before him who bought it from a couple of brothers who bought it from the real Petrol Pete back in the 1950s. But if our Petrol Pete wanted folks to call him something else, he would have changed the name of the station."

Betty couldn't argue with that logic.

"Thanks for helping me, Mizz Bell," Lily Grace said when Betty passed through the gate. "I can do it myself, but Mama doesn't like me being out here alone." She was dressed in stained jeans, square-toed boots, and a calico, long-sleeved shirt.

"You're all grown up now, Lily Grace. You can call me *Betty*."

"Yes, ma'am."

Betty started to laugh but thought better of it. She said, "I've never collected eggs before. I'm not sure what to do." She imagined dreamy soft chickens the size of a newborn baby, a five-pound feathery fluff. When she'd stroke it, it'd even coo like a baby and snuggle deeper into her arms. Rusty red chickens, perhaps, or white birds with comical, yellow stick-legs.

As soon as Lily Grace closed the gate, a giant monster bird, about thirty inches tall, steel gray with death-dagger claws and squawking like the armageddon was nigh, charged Betty. Its head was high, chest out, wings hunched up like a punk itching for a fight. The beast let out a raspy shriek. "What is *that?* Some kind of emu? And what's it doing?" She took a step back.

"Why, it's a rooster, Mizz Betty. He's just being protective. Act like you're not here to do any harm, and he'll leave you alone." She pulled a ball cap from her hip pocket and donned it, stringing her glossy, chestnut hair through the hole in the back.

The sun peered over the treetops and lit Elrod's field. The rooster drew closer.

Betty took another step back. She bit down on a scream.

"Mizz Betty, are you alright?" Lily Grace returned

to Betty and hooked an arm around her waist.

Betty forced her feet forward. Stickers collected on her shoes. "I didn't expect chickens to be so big."

They passed an ancient Ford pickup truck with a rusty roof, missing rear bumper, and new mud tires. There were egg crates in the back.

"Elrod bred his tall Aseels with beefy Brahmas," Lily Grace said. "The Aseels will fight any predator, which keeps the girls safe, and even if one of the roosters loses a fight with a fox or bobcat or something, the ruckus will be so loud the girls will go hide in safety inside in their coops."

Betty didn't like thinking about animals fighting one another, but she supposed that was the way of nature.

"Just stick with me," Lily Grace said as she led Betty past the rooster. "Ol' Brutus knows me. I ain't a threat. If I says you ain't trouble, Brutus will accept you."

They moved toward a rusty horse trailer with hinged shutters covering the windows. Once there, Lily Grace opened the door, and they entered the dusky interior. It smelled like turned earth and very slightly like vinegar. It was also very tidy.

"I had expected more chicken poop and, well, flies," Betty said.

"Elrod takes care of the droppings inside the coops, and the girls take care of the flies." She giggled. "But Elrod's pretty good at snatching flies too."

"With his hands? That's amazing."

"No, not with his hands. He does it just like the girls do."

She can't mean that he... Betty looked for signs of

humor coming from Lily Grace and saw none.

"But you's right about Elrod." A smile brightened her already beautiful face. "He's amazing."

Hens hopped down the roosting ladder at the far end of the trailer like a waterfall of feathers. They weren't as tall as Brutus, but just as beefy, and wore feathery coats of gray, brown, and every combination in between, some with white or blue flecks. They pecked at Betty's shoes and the hay-strewn floor surrounding her feet.

Lily Grace pointed to a metal container on a high shelf. "Grab that tin directly," she said, pronouncing the last word *DIE-rectly* with the small-town Southern lilt Betty had never mastered though she'd lived in Tulip three-plus decades. "Scatter a handful of feed on the floor, and they'll quit pecking you. We gotta do it anyway because the girls will stir up the hay, air it out some. You don't have to change it as often if you keep it aired out."

Betty reached her hand in the tin and pulled out a fist of seeds. Not seeds. "Is this rice?" she asked. They looked like oversized grains of rice with pointy ends and black stripes circling the middle. She threw them on the floor. The hens left off pecking her shoes and started scratching through the hay on the floor.

"It's dried fly larvae." Lily Grace held out a pickle bucket for Betty. "Take this. I already put hay in the bottom to cushion the eggs." Turning to the first cubby, Lily Grace slid her arm along the side wall of the compartment while talking softly to the bird occupying it. "If there's a setter in a nest box, just coax it out like this, see?"

Betty nodded. "I thought there'd be more cubbies,

uh, nest boxes."

A muscled, round, gray beachball of a bird dropped out of the first cubby. "Elrod keeps only one row of nest boxes on each side of the coop. It keeps the girls happy. They'll get all stressed out if they're nesting one atop the other." She held up an egg, one of two that were in the cubby. "This here's a shiny egg, see that?"

Betty nodded.

"There's a little break, and it's done leaked out." She threw the shiny egg out the door. "The girls will eat the broken eggshells and get some calcium."

Steeling herself, Betty reached into a nest box on the opposite side of the coop and cupped her hand behind the hen.

It squawked and flapped its wings in the tight space and pecked at Betty's chest and scratched her arm with its considerable claws on its way out.

Betty yelped, surprised at the amount of blood dripping down her arm. She blinked away the pain and with shaky fingers picked up the solitary, cream-colored egg.

A hand pressed on her shoulder, and Betty yelped.

"I didn't mean to make you jump, Mizz Betty."

Betty looked at Lily Grace, unsure of what to say.

"It's just I can tell you're scared." (Again, the beautiful lilt, Lily Grace pronounced *scared* with a hard T at the end.) "Mizz Williams never told me you ain't been around chickens before." She set aside her pickle bucket, picked up the hen that had just scratched Betty, and sat down in the doorway of the coop with the chicken in her lap. "Come sit next to me."

Betty flinched. *In the hay and fly larvae?*

Lily Grace patted the floor beside her. The hen's feet rested on her thighs, its head held high like Brutus had done, except the hen's sickle-beak was pointed right at Lily Grace's throat.

Without any sudden motions, Betty lowered herself on the floor with her legs dangling over the edge of the doorway.

"You ever have a cat, Mizz Bell?"

"Yes." Technically, it was her first foster parents' cat.

"Just pet Henrietta here like you was trying to get a cat to purr."

Betty reached over and stroked the bird. To her surprise, there was no firm flesh beneath her hand. The soft goodness of the hen's feathers ran deep and swirled between her fingers. It was like reaching into a warm bath. Nonetheless, she didn't allow her hand to get too near the bird's claws.

"Now, keep petting Henrietta and watch her eyes." Lily Grace raised the pitch of her voice and said sweet nothings to the bird.

Henrietta's pupils grew so big the irises all but disappeared. Her eyes quickly returned to normal, but before they did, Betty saw Lily Grace's reflection in the black depth of the bird's eyes. Henrietta's pupils expanded and contracted twice more.

"That there's *pinning*, Mizz Betty. It's a chicken's way of saying she loves you."

Surely Betty would think of something to say later, something to capture the amazing human-bird (country-girl-and-*vicious*-bird) bonding, but all she could think of for now was, "Wow." And "You're quite smart, Lily Grace."

Bottomless eyes mirror
A steel-boned woman, fortified muscles
Swathed in Grace and calico

The next two coops were easier. The nest boxes had back doors. Betty could stand outside the coop, open the shutter-like back door, and nudge the tail end of the hen just a bit in order to get to the eggs.

Brutus finally ignored Betty as she and Lily Grace made their way to the final coop, a delightful gingerbread house on wheels that Lily Grace's brother had made for an Eagle Scout project "on account of Elrod rescuing some Shamo chickens from an unethical breeder, and they needed a place to roost at night," Lily Grace explained.

"Elrod rescues birds?" *Sylvia would have loved this.*

"Shamos are fightin' birds, and Elrod, being the kind of man he is, couldn't abide by that, so he traded his flatbed trailer for the lot of 'em."

Lily Grace opened the main door. "I'll do the right side while I'm here." Betty went around the left side of the coop to access the back doors.

"But it was only for a short time," Lily Grace continued. "Shamos aren't good layers. They're raised for eating." *Eatun.* "Elrod–like I said, he's a special kind of man–found a little Mennonite farm in Gaines County with ethical butchering practices."

Betty gingerly placed two eggs, one tan and one spotted, in her bucket. "How does one ethically butcher a chicken?"

Lily tossed a broken egg out the door. "Are you

sure you wanna know? It's clean and quick-like, but you folks from Tulip proper are kinda squeamish."

"No, no." She shook her head vigorously. "I don't need to know."

Lily Grace emerged from the coop with a couple dozen eggs in her bucket. "I'll help you finish up this side."

They were inching closer to a mound of loose dirt behind the coop. It was about seven feet long and three feet wide.

"What's that pile of dirt?" Betty asked.

"Don't give that no mind, Mizz Bell."

Goosebumps rose on Betty's arms despite the morning's rising temperature. Was she standing a mere fifteen yards from Mr. Smith's grave?

"Dadgummit!"

"What's wrong?" Betty asked.

"I dropped a perfectly good egg to the inside of the coop." She stomped around the corner, presumably to go pick up the broken egg and toss it outside.

Now was Betty's chance. She darted over to the grave-shaped mound and kicked the dirt with her toe. She screamed.

Chapter 7

colony of ants
limbs a blur antenna high
stingers poised to strike

Fire ants, everywhere. Betty screamed again. She bopped and shimmied her way backwards.

"I told you" (*tolt* you) "to stay away from that ant hill." Lily Grace grabbed Betty's pickle bucket. "Don't break the eggs."

Betty flicked and brushed at her legs until long after nothing remained on her skin but a couple of red dots.

Lily Grace's stern countenance shifted to a smile, then she giggled. "You shoulda seen the way you danced, Mizz Betty."

Laughing along with Lily Grace, Betty took her bucket back and returned to the task at hand. She looked at the sweet, young woman gathering eggs from the final nest box, and she thought about the goofy, skunk-stew man who lived on this property. Neither were capable of murder.

Somewhere in the process of gathering eggs at the

gingerbread coop, Betty was thinking how the hens' eggs in her bucket would never produce chicks. At one point she told the hens, "We have more in common than you think." An errant tear dripped down her cheek.

> *My nest of hay*
> *Cushioned with feathers gray*
> *My egg, if fertilized, young life*
> *If not, my barren sister cries*

Betty brushed the tear away and focused on why she agreed to come help gather eggs. "Do you have a boyfriend, Lily Grace?"

"Fernando took me to the Sonic in Eastland a few times. One time, they got his order wrong." She scrunched up her face. "He can be meaner than sin. I don't go out with him no more, and that made him real mad."

Betty found one more egg then closed the access door to the nest boxes. "Yes, I overheard him on the phone four weeks ago. He was angry at someone, a woman, apparently. Must have been you."

"Four weeks ago?" Lily Grace said. They were making their way toward the rusty pickup truck. "No, I broke up with him last week. I tell you what, though. Something was bothering him about a month ago. He wouldn't tell me what it was, but he sure was antsy."

I've got to find out who made him so angry. Maybe it was Sylvia.

They transferred the eggs to the trays. "Why is this tray blue?" Betty asked.

"It goes straight to the Creamery. They ain't kiddin' when they says they use fresh ingredients."

"And the other trays?"

"I'll take them to the processor about two miles south of here. They buy 'em, clean 'em with baby wipes, heat-pasteurize 'em, pack 'up, and deliver them to The Tulip Grocer."

Lily Grace returned the pickle buckets to the first coop while Betty waited. When the young woman returned, she said, "Get in the truck, Mizz Betty. I'll take you to town when I stop by the Creamery."

Betty cast her gaze about the field. Chickens were exploring, scratching the ground, pecking. One was in a sand pit, rolling around and cleaning her feathers. *Good heavens, LB and I have been eating Elrod's free range eggs all this time and didn't know it.* She must have looked too long and too hard at the hens because Brutus charged her again. She scurried into the passenger seat and slammed the door just as Brutus took a chunk of rust out of the door panel.

"Ha!" Betty said, glaring through the side window at the beast. "I closed the door with perfect timing."

"Mizz Betty," Lily Grace said with a scolding tone, "I'm surprised at you. Only God has perfect timing."

"True, Lily Grace, true."

They drove the short distance to the gate. Since Brutus had wandered off, Betty hopped out and opened the gate for the truck to pass through.

"I'm sorry about Brutus," Lily Grace said after Betty climbed back in. "But I thank you for your help, and I hope you had a nice time. I love it here. I look forward to helping Elrod every day."

Betty couldn't help but notice the way Lily Grace said Elrod's name. "You're awfully fond of Elrod, aren't you?"

Color rose in the young woman's cheeks. "I keep hoping Elrod might ask me to go for a walk or something, but he doesn't seem to notice me other than to notice I'm good with his girls." She put the truck in gear, and it chugged onto the road with a metallic wail and a clatter.

Betty checked the side mirror to see if any pieces of Ford had fallen off.

Betty looked sidelong at Lily Grace's youthful curves, slender legs, and flawless skin. There was no way Elrod hadn't noticed her. "Maybe he's shy. Do you happen to have a Red Raiders tee shirt?"

Lily Grace nodded. "That's where my brother Cody goes to college. He's an odd duck. He always said he wanted to escape this place. I don't know what for."

"You might try wearing that tee shirt next time you see Elrod."

When Betty checked the mail that afternoon, she found a pastel envelope with gold-leafed drawings of rattles and bottles and safety pins around the border. An invitation to a baby shower.

She slouched back inside the house.

When it had become clear she'd never be a mother, Betty had sworn off baby showers.

She didn't recognize the name on the return address. "Mimi Anne Ott?" It had to be Odessa Lynn's mother.

When Betty opened the invitation, she didn't recognize the mother's name, either. Good, she didn't feel obligated to go.

She went to her office to get her phone and relay her regrets to the hostess, but an incoming call arrived first.

Adhira.

"Hello, Adhira." The sweat glands under Betty's armpits sprang to life.

"*Of Dust and Daisies*, talk to me, Betty."

"Fine!" Betty answered a bit too quickly. She hoped Adhira wouldn't notice.

"Good to hear. Let's pitch a people collection next."

Betty tossed the baby shower invitation on her desk and sighed. "I'm not done with *Of Dust and Daisies*." She picked up a pad of paper and started fanning her face.

"You sound blue. Do I need to send chocolate?"

"No, I–"

"Good. Now that we're past the pandemic, readers will be looking for less nature and more people."

"Oh, I see."

"I could send a bag of those coffee beans you like so much," Adhira said.

"Really, I'm fine. It's just that I got a baby shower invitation in the mail, and you know I don't like baby showers." Her sweat pores were full-on fountain now, so she flipped on the ceiling fan and stood underneath it.

"Perfect, go! You can do your observation-thing. Take some notes for future poems. Get the gears turning."

Betty stared at her phone. How do people keep up with Adhira? "Should I finish *Of Dust and Daisies* if people are looking for human-centered poetry?"

"I said *will be* looking for, Betty. We've got to stay ahead of the game. Are you sure you don't want the coffee?"

"No, really, Adhi–"

"Great! Bye, then."

A weight settled in Betty's stomach. If she went to the baby shower, she'd probably be sad for days. *Lord, forgive me. I know I should be happy for someone else without feeling sorry for myself.*

"What's wrong?" LB said.

Betty spun, startled. "I didn't know you were standing there."

He stepped closer. "I heard your voice. Flustered. Were you talking to Jacqueline or Adhira? Because they both have that effect on you."

"Adhira. She wants me to go to a stupid baby shower."

LB dropped his gaze. He was silent for a moment. "That's rough. Look, why don't I take you on a coffee date to make up for it, that coffee place in Eastland."

Betty looked back and forth between her computer and LB. "I better not. I'm behind."

"Well," he said, "I'll let you get back to work."

She eyed her phone. Squaring her shoulders, she dialed the RSVP number on the invitation to accept. Adhira was right. It'd be a great opportunity to people-watch.

Chapter 8

Goodbye, my dear
I will love you impulsively
A postcard from the corner
Another from the station

Betty caught up with Juan on the way into class the third Saturday of July. Her plan was to ask the students if they had any idea where Mr. Smith could have gone. But without letting on that a fellow student was dead, of course.

Juan's steps were long and springy, his shoulders loose. He was obviously and blissfully unaware that one of his peers had been bludgeoned to death with a sledgehammer. Betty's eyes threatened to tear up, but she briefly turned into the wind to dry them. She copied his loose stride and tried to appear relaxed.

"Hey, Mrs. Bell."

"Juan, I was wondering, do you know where Mr. Smith works, or is he retired?"

"The junior high science teacher? Duh, he works in the junior high wing, but not in the summer. He's not as good as Mama Teach. She makes chemistry fun. I might have sort of flunked her class so I could take it again this year."

He reached the door and started to go through first, but then stepped back and held the door.

"No, I mean Sylvia's grandfather Mr. Smith." She waited for him to follow her through the doorway.

Juan scrunched up his face. "Mrs. Bell." He dropped his face and shook his head as if laughing at her. "Her name is Bridget Ewell, not Smith."

"Of course, your classmate Bridget, but–"

"And the old dude knows about me. It's all cool. We're on the up-and-up, see?"

Betty slowed down. How could Juan have gotten the freckle-faced cheerleader mixed up with a missing Goth girl. Didn't he even bother to learn Sylvia's name?

Betty jogged back outside and went through the same, awkward conversation with Darlene.

"Who, Mrs. Bell?" Darlene shifted her notebook from one Rubenesque hip to the other.

"Don't you kids introduce yourselves and chat? Engage in small talk?"

Darlene flipped her hair off her shoulders. "We're cheerleaders, Mrs. Bell. Nothing we do is small."

A few minutes later, Julie said, "I don't know freak-girl's grandfather, but I'm *so* glad she dropped out. I knew she didn't belong in this class. She totally smells like sweat and dresses like a weirdo. Gross."

They were standing on the sidewalk. Jorge and the twins filed past followed by the rest of the front row. Julie was athletic enough to swing a sledgehammer, and she clearly disliked Sylvia, but Julie spoke of Sylvia in the present tense. A clever play on Julie's part, or was she truly innocent? Betty decided on *innocent*. As proven by the girl's poetry, she lacked the self-awareness to alter her speech patterns.

It was time for class to start, no more pulling students aside to talk. She followed Julie into the building. Betty would keep a keen eye on the students. Would any of them cast guilty glances at Sylvia's empty chair? Had any of them frightened Mr. Smith and run him off? Hank, for one, would intimidate anyone with just a look.

She cleared her throat and spoke up. "Today's poem will be a narrative. Tell a story about two people meeting and introducing themselves for the first time." She was winging, having thrown today's lesson plan out the window to the grasshoppers. "Make the strangers' dialogue, the words they speak, show what kind of people they are."

Hank fiddled with something below his desk.

"Put away your phone, Hank."

Red crept up the boy's cheeks, and he dropped his phone in his backpack.

While the kids settled down and wrote, Betty stood against the classroom windows. She knew she'd be silhouetted by the glaring afternoon sky. The kids wouldn't be able to tell where exactly she was looking.

The twins whispered. Bridget looked at the ceiling. Juan wrote then scribbled and wrote again. Julie sighed, and Darlene twirled her pen. No one even glanced at Sylvia's seat.

After ten minutes of this, Betty felt sorry for her young poets. She strode to the front of the classroom. "Hank, let's say a center from the other team locked eyes with you. What would you say?"

Hank laughed. He lowered his voice to a growl and said, "You're mine, pansy."

"See? Those words define you as a competitive athlete. Juan, what would your mother say to your little brother if he hiccupped?"

"She'd get a glass of water and say, 'Quick cup, quick cup, solves a silly hiccup.'"

Betty raised her eyebrows. "Really?"

"Yeah."

"Ah, I see. It runs in the family," she said.

Julie raised her hand. "So, you mean, like, if Hank and I met for the first time, I would say, 'It's totally cool to meet you,' and Hank would say, 'Hello, gorgeous,' because he thinks I'm pretty."

Odessa Lynn rolled her eyes. Betty nodded at Julie but couldn't bring herself to say anything.

"Dude," said Juan, "I get it now."

All of the students went back to work except Hank. His gaze lingered on Sylvia's empty chair.

After class, Betty stopped him, but he said he couldn't talk and hurried off to Julie's convertible. It was comical how he folded his big frame into the passenger seat like a grizzly stuffing himself into a silverware drawer.

Betty would have to figure out another time to speak with the boy. She pursed her lips in thought. He had summer football camp during the week. *Guess who's going for a jog past the football field Monday afternoon.*

Two days later, as the afternoon sun beat down on Tulip, Betty hovered at the edge of the gridiron. Her running shirt clung to her torso. Sweat dripped off her nose. The coach dismissed the red-faced, puffing lot of football players, and she jogged onto the field, intersecting Hank.

"Can't talk now, Mrs. Bell."

"Why not?" The sorry grass beneath their feet was mostly dust and spurweed. She swiped at the sweat blurring her vision.

He sprinted to the endzone, and Betty followed. "I was late," he said when she caught up. "Got twenty wind sprints with granny jumps at the fifty and pushups at the end zones." He finished his pushups and stood.

Betty pointed her chin at another athlete doing exercises. "Was he late, too?"

"Mike? Nah." Hank took off in another sprint. Betty followed and caught him at the fifty while he squatted like a frog then leapt into the air with his hands reaching for the sun. "Mike mouthed off. Burpees and tuck jumps. Sucks to be him."

Hank finished his last granny jump and took off. Again, Betty ran after him.

"About Sylvia," she said as he did his pushups.

"Yeah," he grunted, stood, and took off back toward the fifty.

On his second granny jump, she caught him.

"Did she drop…" He took a gasping breath. "Out of class?"

Was he playing innocent? "You should know."

He took off, his pace slower. She could almost keep up now.

At the end zone, he started his pushups and paused

after the fourth one. "How'd you find out?"

Betty's shoulders sank. She wanted the killer to be caught, but she didn't want it to be Hank. He was a good kid, really. She'd known his parents for years through church. The way Mr. and Mrs. Young put it, Hank and his little sister were delightful kids that never gave them any trouble.

Suddenly, Betty realized she was alone on the field next to a monster of a teenage boy who just admitted in so many words that he killed Sylvia. She glanced over her shoulder. The other players were gone. Just Mike on the far side of the field. Betty tried to relax. Hank wouldn't try anything in front of another player. Besides, forty players plus two coaches saw her come on the field.

They ran to the fifty. "Because," she said, answering his question, "you were the only student who looked at Sylvia's empty seat."

After the second granny jump, Hank fell to his knees and panted. A mist of sweat burst from behind his facemask with every exhale.

"Should you be doing wind sprints with full gear on?"

He resituated himself and jumped. "It's not." He sucked in a breath. "Something." Jump. "Wussy like." Pant, jump. "Cross-country running, no offense." He took off running.

Betty glared after him then sprinted for the endzone, passing him at the ten-yard line. She cocked her weight to one hip. "Tell me about Sylvia, Hank."

He rolled his eyes, and Betty couldn't tell if it was because he was about to pass out or if he was tired of her questions.

"She's cool and smart. Her grandfather is the only family she's got left in the world. And it was only one date." He dropped to a pushup stance. "Not a big deal."

Betty didn't want to think like this, but she said, "And she rejected your advances–"

"No! It wasn't that kind of date." He rested on his knees and took a few breaths before finishing his pushups. "But you gotta keep it quiet anyway, Mrs. Bell."

They ran toward midfield.

"Why? Didn't Mr. Smith approve?" she asked at the fifty when he caught up.

"He was cool with it." He lowered to a squat and started his jumps. "But I got a girlfriend. She wouldn't understand."

"Julie, of course," she said.

He finished his granny jumps, and they took off. Betty waited in the endzone for Hank to stumble in and fall into his pushup stance. "You know," he said after the first pushup. "You're pretty fast for an old lady."

Betty jogged away from the stadium and reviewed what Hank had said. Could she believe the boy? He was physically capable, but after watching him do his punitive wind sprints unsupervised by a coach, Betty had a hard time picturing someone with that much discipline letting his anger get the best of him, especially to the point of attacking a smaller, weaker Sylvia.

Betty paused in a gravel driveway to let a car pass

on the highway.

Of course, Jacqueline was still a possibility. Could her flighty friend really be capable of violence?

Once home, Betty peeled off her sweat-soaked running clothes and hopped in a cool shower, letting the water rinse the dust from the football field and the salty sweat from her eyes. But it didn't rinse away the sorrow over Sylvia's murder. Remembering the drought, Betty kept her shower short.

LB was waiting with a towel in hand when she stepped out. He wrapped it around her, and she sank into his arms. Something about a loved one's embrace made even dark days feel better.

"You got a postcard from Fort Worth," he said. "I left it on the kitchen table. Terrible handwriting."

Betty scratched her brain, trying to remember whom she knew in Fort Worth. She had spent her last two years of high school in the city but hadn't been back much except for speaking engagements.

Betty got dressed and called Flora, catching her up on everything Hank had said. "What do you think?"

"I think," Flora said, "it's time for *Glitter my Eyelashes.* Catch ya later, hon." She hung up.

"You're no help," Betty said to her blank screen. She made her way to the living room and settled into the upholstered chair by the tea table. She was midway through her current read, *The Old Man and the Sea.* LB was already in his recliner, wisps of his thinning hair drooping across his forehead. He was reading *The Martian.*

"Impossible," he grunted at the text then turned the page.

They read in companionable silence.

Gradually, the room darkened with the setting sun. Crickets began their song. She flipped on the lamp and kept reading. Santiago, the old man, spent most of the book philosophizing about age. *Why do old men wake so early? Is it to have one longer day?*

Betty looked up from her book and laughed out loud. No, she thought with a glance at her husband who woke at all hours of the night, it's because their prostates are giving them trouble and they have to go pee again.

LB eyed her. "Funny book, eh?"

Smiling, Betty said, "It certainly brings out the funny moments in life."

After a few more pages, Betty set aside her book and retrieved the postcard. She held it under the reading lamp. The image was that of a one-story motel, an older style of architecture, from the 1960s perhaps. Welcome to Fort Worth MotoLodge, the city's premier motor inn.

Motor inns went out with house calls from doctors. LB was right about the handwriting. It was upright cursive rather than slanted. Broken pen marks showed where the author had hesitated. Most bizarre, though, was the message once Betty deciphered it: *Leave the Sylvia problem alone or else.*

Betty's mouth went dry. "LB," she said, "I think I've stirred up a hornet's nest." She called Miller.

Miller was off duty and didn't live but two blocks over. He said he'd be there in less than a minute.

The postcard frightened Betty, but it piqued her curiosity, too, and she wanted more time to study it. She took a picture of the front and back and finished just as the doorbell rang.

While Betty explained to Miller about interviewing

the kids as to Mr. Smith's whereabouts and learning of Hank's date with Sylvia, LB stood with his hands in his pockets rattling his keys, rocking up on his toes, and pressing his lips together. Usually, only Flora could get him this rattled.

Betty wasn't ready to point a finger at Jacqueline yet, so she kept quiet about Sylvia and her supposed blackmailing. Actually, Bartholemew had just as much a financial reason to want Sylvia out of the picture as Jacqueline did.

That is, of course, if Sylvia really was Jacqueline's illegitimate child and if the girl really did try to blackmail Jacqueline. Definitely too many unanswered questions to be pointing fingers at the Ivys.

LB cleared his throat. "Did you narrow down the time of death?"

"Larry." Miller scowled.

"It'd compromise the investigation if he told you that," Betty said to her husband. "Right, Miller?"

"Darn straight," he said.

"But," Betty continued, "I do have an almost two week window between classes to narrow it down." She sat in her reading chair and tapped the side of her head. Bartholomew's sales trips were often weeks long. Had Bartholemew even been in town at the time? "Maybe he can still be crossed off as a suspect," said out loud on accident.

"I can't say whether or not Hank is still a suspect."

She hadn't meant Hank. She had meant Bartholemew. Her heart felt heavy in her chest. Of course, she, too, had considered Hank a suspect, but she'd mostly dismissed that notion.

She closed her eyes and slowly shook her head. He

was so young, such a bright future as a... She wasn't so naive as to think one boy from a small town would make it to the NFL when there were over a million other high schoolers in the States competing for the same few spots. But since she'd gotten to know Hank a little better, how disciplined he was and how hard he practiced, she thought maybe he had a chance.

~

Late afternoon on Tuesday, LB dropped Betty off at the Otts' newly built barndominium home east of Tulip.

She stood at the door, the crunch of LB's tires on gravel receding in the distance. From the property next door came the driving whirr of a pumpjack. Laughter and squeals seeped through the windows and walls of the house. Betty swallowed hard then knocked.

A familiar person, Jacqueline, opened the door.

"Betty? What are you doing here?" Jacqueline's voice conveyed shock though her Botoxed face registered only faint surprise. She was dressed in a finely tailored linen suit that probably cost more than a month of LB's salary. "I didn't think you'd ever... well, bless your heart," she said, grabbing Betty by the arm and yanking her inside.

They were in the kitchen half of a kitchen and living room combo. The laughter and chatter stopped. Heads turned in Betty's direction, and she felt like a fish in a lighted fishbowl.

A woman Betty didn't know, but who looked suspiciously like Odessa Lynn even through a layer of makeup thick enough to plow through, took the wrapped gift Betty was holding and exchanged it for a champagne flute. The opaque, gold plastic party glass shined like 24-carat jewelry.

"Odessa Lynn just *loves* your class," said the woman. "She'd be here if it weren't for cheer camp."

Betty tried to give the flute back. "No thanks, I don't..." Betty started, but the woman had already turned away, and the party noise resumed.

Jaqueline led Betty past the refrigerator where a photo of Odessa Lynn in her Bulldogs cheerleading uniform was held in place by a miniature football magnet. Natural curls framed her face instead of the braids she wore now.

The living room was set up like a golden baby palace. There was gold wrapping paper with embossed baby faces taped over the walls. Metallized plastic baby bottles graced the television console. On the dining table dividing the kitchen from the living room, there were donuts dusted with gold flakes. The donuts sat between baked beans and chicken nuggets on one side and potato salad and buffalo wings on the other.

"Are those edible?" Betty asked, pointing to the donuts.

"Of course, silly. Gold goes right through you." Jacqueline said.

Hundreds of glistening, translucent streamers spiraled from the living room ceiling. They looked like crepe paper, but–

"Ladies!" Jacqueline raised her voice, interrupting Betty's thoughts. "Let me introduce you to Betty Bell."

What are those streamers?

Laugher slowly faded, conversations dimmed.

"Mimi Anne said you were coming," said a woman with hair even taller than Jacqueline's. It looked stiff enough to use as a motorcycle helmet. "Will you autograph my book?" She held out a pen and a copy of *Of Canyons and Kayaks*.

"Not now, Barbie May," Jacqueline said, pushing the woman aside. "I have to introduce Betty to all the ladies." She spun Betty about and gestured at the crowd. "Of course, you know Pastor Bethany. She brought the baked beans."

Pastor Bethany was leaning awkwardly on the back of a recliner. Her eyes were glassy, and she raised her champagne flute at Betty.

"Pastor Bethany," Betty said with a gasp, "have you been drinking?" Although Betty herself didn't drink, she had no problem with responsible alcohol consumption. It's just that Pastor Bethany was *staunchly* anti-alcohol.

She raised her champagne glass at Betty. "Unfetter your anguish, little lamb. It's only sparkling cider."

Betty took a sip from her own glass. "Um, Pastor Bethany–"

"Anyway," continued Jacqueline, "this is Wanda." Jacqueline nodded toward a woman on the couch. "You can see her handiwork on your husband."

Before Betty could ask what Jacqueline was implying, Jacqueline explained. "She's Wanda the *barber*. And Fernando's sister."

Betty perked up. "I'd love to chat with you, Wanda." Maybe Wanda could tell her what had made Fernando so angry the day Betty overheard him on the phone.

"Moving on," Jacqueline said, "the woman in the prostitute heels still trying to get you to sign her book is Barbie May Day." She shooed Barbie May yet again. "Now please meet Savannah Honey Cooter, Margaret

Jo Johnston, Sally Jane Zimmermann, Mimi Anne Ott, Mary Sue Pickles, Mary *June* Pickles, and Joan." Jacqueline leaned in and whispered, "Joan's not from around here."

Betty was woefully underdressed in her walking shorts and church flats among the skirts, heels, and Instagram-worthy makeup.

Betty recognized Savannah Honey, Homer and Elrod's baby sister, from Midtown Creamery, and Margaret Jo was obviously the mother-to-be. And the Pickles sisters went to Tulip Community Church though they hung out with a younger crowd. In fact, Betty was the oldest person in the room and old enough to be several of the women's mothers.

Betty combed her gray hair into place with shaky fingers and nodded hello at everyone. She sidled away from Jacqueline and took a spot on the couch next to Wanda.

"Hello," said the woman. She had Fernando's long eyelashes and broad smile.

"It's nice to meet you, Wanda. I'm awfully fond of your brother." Betty's eye spasmed. She tittered. "Um, has that certain issue from a month ago cleared up?" It wasn't a very smooth attempt at plying information. Betty hoped the woman was too tipsy to notice.

Wanda rolled her eyes and spilled a bit of champagne in the process. She was plenty tipsy. "Oh that. He was mad as all get out at Mom."

"Whatever for?"

"She rented the old Sanchez place to some man and his daughter."

Or granddaughter.

Betty almost spilled her own champagne when she

realized what Wanda was saying. "Your mother owns the old Sanchez place?"

"You didn't know her maiden name is *Sanchez?*" Wanda pivoted in her seat, and her tone turned more conspiratorial. "Fernando thought Mom didn't charge enough and the renters took advantage of her." She drained her glass and stood, planting her feet wide as if on a rocking boat. "But I say no one's lived there my whole life, so even a little rent money is better than letting it sit empty. Especially since they were gonna fix it up, make it livable."

After Wanda headed off for another refill, Betty retrieved her notebook from her purse. But how was she going to take notes in her notebook while holding a glass of champagne? The coffee table was piled high with pastel-wrapped gifts, so she put her drink on the nearest windowsill then began to write.

A black-haired woman leans her head toward the mother-to-be, crumbs of advice tumbling from her lips. The pregnant woman nods.

The slender woman stands with one hand cradling an elbow, the other hand cradling champagne.

A petite woman holds her champagne glass at an angle. Her eyes are focused not on her drink but on the food table, on the donuts. She chews her lower lip. Her gaze scans the room, and I look away. When I look up again, she has a donut in her mouth.

"If that's what you got Margaret Jo's baby, you can find your own ride home." The speaker's eyeglasses are round coins reflecting the gold decor of the room. The pages of my notebook have taken on a gold hue too.

"How'd that get in here?" Jacqueline's voice.

"Margaret Jo, get your fly swatter."

The petite woman flicks a flake of gold from her blouse.

The preacher burps. Her cheeks–

Someone screamed, jolting Betty. She dropped her notebook and looked toward the noise.

Barbie May was thrashing about in the kitchen. "I'm allergic to bees!" she yelled.

Margaret Jo smacked the offending creature with the fly swatter, but Barbie May kept thrashing her arms about and backing away from the kitchen. She ended up in the living room area.

"Barbie May," Jacqueline yelled, "you can't go over there in your prostitute shoes!"

It was too late. Streamers stuck to Barbie May's hair like–

Fly strips, Betty finally realized.

They hung from Barbie May's crisp hairdo like coiled snakes from a coconut. She twisted about and swatted the air.

"I told you not to wear your prostitute shoes," Jacqueline said. "You look possessed."

"Possessed?" Pastor Bethany snapped to attention. She reached for her purse on the floor next to the recliner and whipped out a Bible. Brandishing it like a weapon, she yelled, "Restrain her, sisters. I'm going to war!"

"The whole scene devolved into a wrestling match of painted up, fancied up prosti–I mean, women," Betty said to LB.

It was evening, and Betty was back home. The two of them were getting ready for bed.

"And poor Barbie May," she said, "her wig came off. That monofilament hair will never be the same." Betty had been somewhat comforted to learn that it wasn't real hair doing the style tricks that Barbie May's hair was doing when the two of them were first introduced.

Judging by his snickers, LB was clearly enjoying the story.

Betty shook her head. "Hush up, LB." She shook her finger at him. "It was a horrible, horrible sight."

He let out a guffaw, climbed under the covers, and said, "Is that when you carried Pastor Bethany outside?"

"She was cork high and bottle low and needed rescuing–from herself, mostly. I grabbed both of our purses and slung her over my shoulder. I called you from the driveway."

Betty knelt and said a prayer for Mr. Smith, wherever he was. Pastor Bethany, too. The poor thing was going to be mortified if she remembered any of it.

"LB," she said after the lights were out, "do you think Fernando could get mad enough at his mother's supposed lack of business acumen to take it out on her renters?"

His only answer was a gentle snore.

Chapter 9
from humble cheese mold
antimicrobial gold
Al Fleming's biome

The horn startled Betty, and she dropped her book bag on the side of the road. Her heart leapt into high speed. A blue Blazer pulled over across the road and honked again.

"Will you stop that, Flora?" she yelled at the car. As her heart settled down, she knelt to pick up her spilled papers before another hot gust of wind tossed them about.

"Honestly, Flora, you make me feel like the new kid in school all over again." When she had first met Tilly, the girl snatched Betty's textbooks and homework from the crook of her elbow and tossed them on the school lawn. But that was before Tilly learned Betty was a runner, too. They eventually became teammates and friends.

Flora rolled down her window. "I know who killed Sylvia!"

Betty stood. "You do?" Her heart shifted to

overdrive again. She looked both ways, ran across the road, then climbed in the passenger side.

Flora pulled back on the road. "Wanda, you know, from the barbershop?" Betty nodded. "Yes, but stop looking at me. Keep your eyes on the road."

"Wanda was cutting Bill Ramsbottom's hair–you know he always looks so darn good with her buzz cuts– and Bill said Charlie said he was at The Tulip Grocer."

Betty clutched the sides of her seat. "You're drifting!"

After a slight jerk to the wheel, Flora continued. "Well, not *in* the store, but in the parking lot, and he saw–"

"We turn left up here. You know I'm going to class, right?"

"Bill, no *Charlie*–my brain doesn't want to let go of that image of Bill with a buzz–Charlie said Hank and Sylvia's grandfather were fighting in the parking lot."

"Put your turn signal on, Flora," Betty said. "But everyone says Mr. Smith is a slight, elderly man. How could he fight Hank?"

"Well, Wanda didn't say that Bill said that Charlie said it came to blows. It could have been a heated exchange of words. Although if Charlie was doing the fighting instead of Mr. Smith, well, you know how everything gets Charlie mad as a box of frogs." They pulled into the school parking lot. "So that proves it. Hank killed Sylvia."

Betty let go of the death grip on her passenger seat and turned toward Flora. "I don't follow," she said in a flat voice.

"Don't you see?" Flora's hands grew animated as

she talked. "Mr. Smith was angry about Hank dating Sylvia, so Hank followed him home and…" She made a slicing motion across her throat. "But Sylvia was a witness, so Hank had to kill her, too."

A long sigh seeped from between Betty's lips. "Then where is Mr. Smith's body?"

"Um." Flora pursed her lips as if in thought. She snapped her fingers. "Easy, Hank dumped it in Hunter's Shirt Creek. It runs through the back of his parents' place."

Hunter's Shirt and all the other creeks in the county were bone dry right now. "Flora, you're my best friend." *And you're an idiot.* "Thanks for the ride." She climbed out of the car.

One thing for sure, though, she'd have to speak to Hank after class. He had claimed that Mr. Smith was fine with his granddaughter dating the hulky football player.

"I miss Mama Teach," Darlene announced as soon as Betty had called the class to order.

Juan rested his chin on the heels of her hands. "Yeah, she makes science cool."

Betty clenched and unclenched her fist. How could she compete with a woman like Mama Teach? "Tell you what," Betty said to the class. "You remember what a haiku is, right?"

"*Cinco-siete-cinco,*" said Sebastian.

Betty folded her arms and looked at him.

"Five-seven-five syllables," he said.

"And haikus are about nature," added Bridget.

With a nod at the girl, Betty said, "Sci-kus are haikus about science instead of nature. In honor of Mama Teach, why don't we write sci-kus today? What science-y topics could we explore?"

"Oh! I know, I know!" Julie waved her hand. "All the angle thingies that make a diamond sparkle."

Juan drummed his pen on his desk. "Or, like, migrating vibrating particles."

"You're so smart, Juan," murmured Bridget as she gazed up at her tall crush.

"Space exploration," said Darlene.

"A ranunculus under a microscope," said Hank.

Julie turned around. "A what?" she asked him.

"How about penicillin under a microscope?" said Jorge.

After dismissing the class, Betty asked Hank to stay in order to "discuss a little matter."

Julie wrapped her arm around Hank's elbow. "I'll stay with you, hunky man. I mean, anything she can say to you, she can say to me, right?"

A closed-lipped smile spread across Hank's face. "Yeah, sure." He looked at Betty with pleading eyes.

"I just wanted to know if *ranunculus* was a word of German origin," Betty said, slick as a whistle. Her eye spasmed. More like slick as pond scum.

Julie seemed to buy it, though, because she grinned up at Hank's face.

"It's Latin, ma'am."

"Oh, Hank, you're a total genius. A ranun-whatever is a fishing boat, right?"

Betty smiled at the couple. "That's all I needed. Thank you, Hank."

Watching them leave, Betty figured she'd have to plan another jog near the football field come Monday afternoon.

It was cool enough Sunday morning that LB suggested they leave the car and walk to church. "I hope Bartholomew is in town," he said. They held hands as they strolled. It was nearly eighty degrees already, but after weeks of three-digit heat, eighty felt good.

"No," Betty replied, "he's out of town."

"The choir's so bad without him it's sinful."

"LB!"

"A *din* of iniquities." He laughed at his own joke.

Flora was climbing out of her Blazer when they crossed the side lawn of the church into the parking lot. She was muttering something and slammed her door.

"Flora," said Betty as they approached, "what's wrong?"

"I'm so dang hungry!"

LB let go of Betty's hand. "Hunger is the result of a hormone called ghrelin," he said to Flora. "It rises during periods of food deprivation. Did you eat breakfast?"

The woman growled.

Patting LB on the shoulder, Betty said. "Why don't

you go on in, dear, before my best friend punches you in the throat? I'll be there in a minute."

With a shrug, he turned and walked toward the building.

"Well, did you eat breakfast?" Betty asked, repeating LB's question.

Flora shook her head. "It's the hottest new thing. I can eat whatever I want between noon and midnight as long as I don't eat a stitch between midnight and noon."

Betty's eyes narrowed. "What did you eat at 11:55 last night?"

"A bowl of tomato soup, an apple, two saltines, and one plateful of brownies."

Betty moaned. "Flora—"

"But I finished before midnight, no cheating!" Her stomach rumbled.

Betty glanced at the front door. "Pastor Bethany's probably waiting for us. Let's get in there." As the two women headed for the door, Betty said a silent prayer for her friend. Betty had never been concerned about her own weight and didn't know anything about dieting, but a plateful of brownies didn't seem like the right way to go about it.

Flora motioned Betty to lean down. "Did you talk to Hank?" she whispered in Betty's ear. "You know, about his argument with Sylvia's grandfather?" She glanced over Betty's shoulder. "There's Miller. Should we go tell him about Hank?"

"No!" Betty practically shouted. Up ahead, the Pickles family, all four of them, turned and looked at Betty. She glanced over at Miller. His eyebrow was raised. Betty lowered her voice. "I haven't talked to Hank yet. I will tomorrow."

That evening over supper Betty talked with LB about what she knew so far. "Apparently, Mr. Smith did not approve of Sylvia going on a date with Hank." She shook her head. "But I can't conceive of a first date–that wasn't really a date, Hank says–ending in murder."

LB served himself a hefty helping of green beans to go with his meatloaf then passed her the bowl. "I have heard of abusive teenage relationships."

Betty shivered at the thought.

"And you know he lied," said LB, "because Hank and Mr. Smith were arguing in the parking lot."

"At least according to Flora according to Charlie according to Bill according to Wanda." Her lips curved in a grin. "I think Flora has the hots for Bill."

"He is an eligible bachelor," LB said, taking a bite of meatloaf.

"Yeah, but can you imagine? Wilhelmina Williams Ramsbottom."

"I can't imagine anyone marrying that woman."

Betty ignored his jab at her best friend. She munched her green beans. The salty, buttery, sweet-grassy taste swirled about her tongue. "LB, your green beans are perfect." Her fork pinged on the Corelle plate as she chased another green bean. "I just don't like to think of one of my students being capable of..." She put down her fork. Suddenly she wasn't hungry anymore.

"Hank didn't do it," LB said.

Betty frowned. "But you just agreed he lied."

"Jacqueline did it. The threatening postcard from Fort Worth came just a couple of days after you said Mr. Stevens sent her there on an errand."

A giggle rose to the surface. "Big haired, manicured, silicone-breasted Jacqueline swinging a sledgehammer? Nah."

"Money makes people do crazy things," LB said.

"She was certainly in a funk the day she went to Fort Worth," Betty admitted. What was Jacqueline going to tell her before Mr. Stevens interrupted? "But I don't think our rich cashier friend is the murderer. Miller has the postcard. He would have arrested her by now if she had sent it."

Besides, Betty had studied the image of the postcard on her phone. Fort Worth MotoLodge was no luxury hotel. There was no way Jacqueline went there. Maybe Betty could take the bus to Fort Worth and ask the motel staff about Jacqueline, just to prove it wasn't her that sent the postcard. To prove she had nothing to do with Sylvia's murder.

"C'mon, LB, we've known Jacqueline ever since she married Bartholemew and moved to Tulip."

"Yup, two decades," LB said.

"She's shallow, flighty, even dimwitted at times, but not cruel. Not violent."

LB reached out and squeezed Betty's hand. "We don't know what goes on behind closed doors, what her private life is like."

Betty huffed. *I'm definitely going to Fort Worth. And I definitely still need to talk to Hank again.*

Monday afternoon, Betty checked the temperature and moaned. Ninety-five degrees. It was going to be a hot run. She had foregone her morning jog in order to catch Hank after football camp.

She went the back way, through the pea gravel footpath in the woods in hopes the drought-stressed trees would still provide adequate shade.

The path opened onto Train Park, a grassy expanse (now mostly sand with tufts of brown grass because of the drought) where an old locomotive sat. Squeals of delight from kids climbing on the iron beast chased her through to the other side of the park where the trail resumed. With relief, she entered the shade.

A quarter mile in, she met Julie running the other way. She was wearing a cheer camp tee.

"Hi Mrs. Bell!" Julie called in passing. The girl was sweating but breathing easily. A chase crowd of red-faced, gasping runners soon followed. They were also wearing cheer camp tees. Next was Odessa Lynn, her braids bouncing about her face. And finally, Darlene. Darlene raised a hand in greeting and let out a noise that sounded like *gah!* Her feet swung to the sides as she ran. Her hands flailed. She was not made to be a runner.

Betty glanced at her watch. She still had ten minutes until football camp let out. Doing a one-eighty, she sprinted past Darlene, and caught up with Odessa Lynn.

"Odessa Lynn, I couldn't help but notice you often

cast less-than-friendly glances at Julie."

"I hate her."

"That's a strong word." Betty dodged a low-lying limb that Odessa Lynn easily passed beneath. "Are you jealous because she dates Hank?"

"OMGosh, no. I'm not even sure he's into girls." She paused and panted. "He's into flowers."

Betty slowed down for the girl. "Just because a guy is interested in... Wait, flowers?" Betty did a mental palm-to-forehead. *Of course. The blackout poem, the ranunculus sci-ku.*

"Ugh, yes, he even took that creep girl on a date to pretend like he's a playa."

"You knew about the date?" They were nearing Train Park, and Betty dreaded going into the sun again.

"Everybody knows except Julie. Everybody's scared to tell her. But not me." Odessa Lynn's mouth was wide open, sucking in air, but she managed a broad, cruel grin. "I can't wait to see her face when I do. I'm just waiting for the right time to do it."

"Odessa Lynn!" Julie called from the edge of the park. "Pick it up. You're going so slow Darlene's about to catch you."

Odessa Lynn rolled her eyes. "I hate her."

"Take care," Betty said as she turned around. Twenty yards later she waved at Darlene in passing then headed for the football field. Obviously, if Odessa Lynn's anger was directed only at Julie and never at Sylvia, then Odessa Lynn had no motive to kill the poor girl. She was never a suspect in Betty's mind to start with, but it was good to cross her off the list just to be sure.

It also meant that Julie was less of a suspect if she

didn't even know about the Hank-Sylvia date.

Didn't know *yet*.

That was going to be a cesspool of teen drama. Betty dodged the same low-lying limb. Betty would have to talk Odessa Lynn out of announcing the news about Hank's date with Sylvia. That was something Hank should tell Julie. But for now–Betty checked her watch–she needed to hurry if she wanted to talk with Hank as he was leaving football camp. She picked up her pace.

Betty burst from the woods at full speed, stretching her legs, pumping her arms. The crunch of pea gravel and dried leaves gave way to the pat-pat of the stadium's parking lot asphalt.

She made for the bleachers, pretending like she was using the benches to stretch.

The athletes were still on the field. Hank apparently spotted her right away. His helmet nodded at her. She motioned with her hand, thumbing her chest then pointing at him. He nodded again and went back to work with the team.

When the coach dismissed the players, Hank took off his helmet and jogged towards Betty. She stood before the bleachers and waited. His pungent odor arrived before he did, a mixture of onions, urine, and old Doritos. He smelled so ripe she wasn't sure his own mother would let him in the house.

Betty got right to the point. If she was talking to a killer, she wanted to get it over with before the coach and other athletes had all left the field. "You were seen arguing with Sylvia's grandfather in the parking lot at the grocery store. I thought you said he was okay with you taking Sylvia on a date."

"It wasn't a date, and he wasn't mad about me *seeing* her." His hair was plastered with sweat, and it dripped from his earlobes. "He was mad about *where* I took her."

"I don't understand."

He shrugged. "I don't, either." He looked left and right then lowered his voice. "I took her to the botanical gardens. Flowers for me. Birds for her. She is *really* into birds."

"The botanical gardens in Weatherford?"

"Shh!" He swiped his palm over his wet face and flung droplets on the ground. "No one can know."

"If it wasn't a date, why can't anyone know?"

He sat on the bleacher, and she sat down next to him.

"Because word might get around to Julie. She wouldn't understand." He cussed. "My future is college football. Gardenias and daisies don't fit into that."

The other players had left the field, their bodies drooping under the stress of their workout. The two coaches, sweaty and red-faced themselves, were still on the field.

"Do your parents know about your floral interests?"

Hank just scrunched up his face and shook his head.

Betty got back to the subject at hand. "I wonder what Mr. Smith had against the botanical gardens."

She pictured the posters on Sylvia's walls. If Mr. Smith had something against birds, why did he let her keep the posters up? Not to mention minors can't get a tattoo without a parent or guardian's consent, so he had to have agreed to that.

"Not the gardens, Mrs. Bell, the city. He didn't like that I took her to Weatherford."

"Interesting. Well, what did you do after you and Sylvia's grandfather had words in the parking lot?"

"Duh, got in my truck–well, my dad's truck–and went home."

Betty stared into the distance. She was trying to remember something Flora had said about Weatherford, but Hank's body odor was making it hard to concentrate. Betty was dripping sweat, too, but she'd only been out thirty minutes, not four hours, not long enough to grow new species of microbes.

They stood. "Hank?"

"Yeah?"

"Go take a shower."

Chapter 10

His index finger traces my wrinkles like a roadmap
Our journey via bus via lust 'til death,
He says I am his speed trap

Tuesday morning, Betty surprised herself by waking up before LB for once. She tiptoed into the kitchen and made coffee. It was a little tricky grinding the beans. She took off her robe and wrapped the electric grinder in the fluffy terry cloth so as not to make too much noise. She wanted to wake him with a pleasant aroma, not a nails-on-a-chalkboard noise of the grinder.

While the coffee was brewing, she slipped outside and retrieved the paper.

LB was waiting for her at the table when she returned. He had a cup of coffee in his hand and took a sip. His nose crinkled, but he smiled and said, "Delicious, Betty."

"Liar." She kissed him and smelled the coffee on his breath. It smelled like diner coffee that had sat out all day. Pulling back, she said, "It's the same beans and the same coffee maker. Why is my coffee never as good as yours?"

Shrugging, he took the paper from her hands, claimed his headlines and puzzles, then tossed the local news and sports on her side of the table.

Betty grabbed a cup of her pitiful coffee and sat down to scan the local news. "Oh no, LB, listen to this."

FARMER'S PET PUMA EATS MAYOR'S BODYGUARD

In a press conference Monday afternoon in the Miami Flowers lobby, Mayor Buford announced the passing of his bodyguard, Roberta. Helper says he's devastated. "We had become friends, Roberta and me. I'm going to miss her keen eye, her quick moves, her sleek, gray feathers." In memory of Roberta, the mayor Superglued 900 of his late bodyguard's feathers on his forest green Cadillac sedan.

Right after breakfast, Betty left the house for the Tulip city hall. She reminded herself that she had taken the bus to Fort Worth before. And survived. All she had to do was catch the thrice daily shuttle from Tulip city hall to the Eastland courthouse, proceed one block west to the Greyhound terminal, and hop on the outgoing bus to downtown Fort Worth.

Surviving the trip with her sanity intact was

another issue. On the shuttle, she closed her eyes and imagined the fifteen-passenger van was a motorboat on the ocean. Once in Eastland, she fought off the resulting sea sickness and boarded the big bus to the metropolis.

The bus exited the terminal, and Betty kept her eyes on the horizon until her nausea faded.

Across the aisle, a little boy about seven or eight had a picture book with a dinosaur on the front resting on his lap. It was emerald green, a hardcover, and worn at the corners.

The bus hit a bump, and Betty's heart rate soared.

Fear thou not for I am with thee be not dismayed fear thou not for I am with thee be not dismayed fear thou not for I am with thee be not dismayed–

The boy ran his thumb around the perimeter of the green cover. He brushed his palm along the title then opened the book. It covered his small lap and poked underneath the armrest and into the aisle.

Fear thou not. Betty's mouth was dry. She checked the mile markers on the side of the interstate. A little more than seventy-five miles. A little less than seventy-five minutes. She took a full breath and let it out slowly.

Using his index finger, the boy traced the words on the page. His lips moved soundlessly. He tilted his head. Turned a page. Index finger. Page. Index finger.

Several minutes must have passed because the boy clapped the book shut and swung his legs. He hugged the book to his chest.

Betty checked the mile markers. Only fifty-five miles left. Her heart still thumped away in her chest, but her mouth was no longer dry. To her amazement, her hands were resting in her lap rather than clutching the armrests.

For I am with thee.

The hotel's address was on her phone. She'd prefer to walk from the bus terminal, but it was too far even for her conditioned legs. The last time she was in Fort Worth, it was just after her forty-first book was released. She spoke to a women's group and sold fifteen copies. LB chauffeured her about. Today she'd have to take an Uber or ride a city bus.

Turns out the Fort Worth city buses were just as frequent and convenient as they were all those years ago when she lived with her third set of foster parents.

The city bus pulled up to the curb. Riding a bus was easier than being a passenger in a car, but Betty's knees still shook when she stepped up into the bus. She brought up her GoPass app and presented her digital ticket to the driver. She collapsed into a window seat and squinted into the late morning sun on the east side of the thoroughfare.

The further up the road the bus went, the more homeless people she saw. The more bedraggled, stumbling pedestrians she saw. This was not a place Jacqueline would go.

Then who sent the postcard?

There, ahead on the right, Fort Worth Motolodge. Betty pulled the cable telling the driver she wanted off at the next stop.

When he pulled over, he paused with his hand on the door lever. "Are you sure, ma'am?"

Betty couldn't speak yet, her fear of traffic still throttling her throat. She nodded.

He opened the door.

Loose gravel, empty beer cans, and cigarette butts populated the motel's parking lot. Metal room doors faced the concrete frontage and exhibited dents, graffiti, and what looked like dried splatters of food. A man slept between the ice machine and the Coke machine. She said a prayer for the man.

Sensing eyes on her back, Betty whipped around, fearing an encounter. No one was immediately behind her, but a hulking figure quickly dashed behind a parked, white economy car and disappeared into the shadows of an adjacent building. It was impossible to see who it was, yet there was a familiarity in the figure's movements.

Whom did she know in Fort Worth nowadays? Her fosters, who weren't in the best of health when they took her in, had long since passed. She pushed aside thoughts of muggers and worse, and she hurried to the lobby.

The receptionist, a brown-skinned woman with short hair, put down her paperback. It was a steamy romance by the looks of the cover. She peered over the Formica counter at Betty. Television voices rattled from a portable set, flies buzzed, and the employee's breath hissed asthmatically from her lungs.

"Check-in's at three o'clock," the woman said. She pursed her lips and looked Betty up and down. With a shrug, the woman said, "Unless you're only checking in for a couple of hours."

Betty's jaw dropped as the meaning became clear. "Young lady," she said, feeling heat rise in her cheeks,

"I'm fifty-eight years old!"

Another shrug. "We get all types."

"No, just, no-no-no." Betty pulled out her phone. She still hadn't shaken the jitters from her two bus rides, and her fingers trembled while scrolling through her images. Betty stopped on a picture of Jacqueline and Bartholemew at a church picnic. "Have you seen this woman?"

"Why?"

"I'm investigating." Betty waited for her eye to twitch, but it didn't. *I guess I really am investigating. I'm a private eye, like Miss Marple!* Her armpits dampened. *I don't like being a private eye.*

The employee leaned toward Betty's phone. "Pfft!"

"Beg your pardon?"

"She wouldn't be seen around here unless she was some kind of church lady."

Betty snapped her phone back. "Is that some kind of insult?"

Again with the shrug. "I'm just saying. People like her come round sometimes, to give out flyers and bottles of water and stuff, but that's all."

"So, you have seen her."

"No, I'd remember that big hair."

Betty made her way back to the city bus stop and read the posted schedule. A fifty-minute wait. She settled down on the bench and reviewed what she'd just learned. Jacqueline hadn't been to the motel and thus hadn't sent the postcard.

Scrolling through her pictures again, she stopped on the postcard. Terrible cursive. Could Mr. Smith have sent it? His advanced age would explain the wild penmanship. But that didn't make sense because Mr. Smith wouldn't warn Betty off the investigation. If anything, he'd want everyone looking for his granddaughter's killer.

Unless he, himself, was the killer.

The hairs on her arms rose. She looked behind her, expecting someone, but nobody was there. The white car was still there. No one was near it, but someone stood across the street in front of a title loan business. A man, Betty thought, because of his height compared to a passing car, but she wasn't sure. The same person from before? She pivoted on the bench to get a better look. He slid into the shadows. She couldn't make out any details, but the person was definitely facing her way. Betty's scalp prickled. Was he staring at her?

She didn't wait to find out.

Betty leapt to her feet and ran in the opposite direction of the title loan business. She hung a right at the next corner. At least the round shape of the man gave her hope that she could outrun someone so ungainly.

Two lovers leaning up against an empty store front broke their embrace and watched her pass. She sprinted the length of the block, jumped over a small dog on a leash, then crossed the road. She darted into a parking garage. Someone called her name.

Had the person who sent the threatening postcard found her? She wasn't stopping.

Exiting on the other side into the business district,

she heard her name again.

"Betty? Betty Glenniford?"

Whoever it was knew her maiden name with the familiarity of friendship. Betty slowed.

"Wait up!" It was a woman.

Betty stopped and turned around, scanning the pedestrians.

"Betty, that *is* you!" A leggy, middle-aged woman was waving and jogging in Betty's direction.

"Theodora?"

The woman nodded. "You're still pretty fast."

Yes, it was Theodora, her high school cross country running teammate. They embraced, and Betty's fear from the foot chase melted in Theodora's arms.

Theodora suggested they have a cup of coffee, and they headed for a coffee shop down the street.

"What are you up to nowadays?" Theodora said as they settled at a table with their drinks. "Wait, you don't have to tell me. You're a famous poet now. I have three of your books." She pulled the napkin from under her cup. "Sign my napkin! Bob–the hubster–will never believe it."

The couple at the next table looked over, and Betty felt her cheeks redden. "My autograph? I'm just small-time, Theodora, not a celebrity."

"Nonsense." She pushed the napkin to Betty's side of the table.

Autograph in hand, Theodora said, "I haven't heard from you since graduation."

Betty was quiet for a moment. "My parents were gone, so I guess with no family to come back to…" Her voice dropped off as the familiar feeling of drifting, of cut loose from the ties that bind, overwhelmed her.

A look of compassion crossed Theodora's face.

"Oh, but I'm fine, really." Betty took a sip of coffee. "I went on to Abilene Christian–"

"I remember," Theodora said. "Tilly was so mad. She thought that scholarship belonged to her."

Betty nodded. "Tilly was the better athlete, but I beat her fair and square at regionals."

Theodora frowned. "I didn't say it at the time–I mean the three of us were so close, like sisters, but I was intimidated by Tilly–I wanted to tell her she was getting overconfident and not training as hard our senior season. It was the first year ACU offered women sports scholarships under Title IX. You'd think she would have trained lights-out."

"She intimidated me, too. She was built like a tank and was protective of us like a big sister, but a *bossy* big sister." Betty tried to laugh at the memories, but it came out as a sigh. She picked at the rim on her paper coffee cup then shrugged. "That was a long time ago. We're all adults now."

They exchanged phone numbers and chatted a little longer until Betty said she had to leave. "I have to snag a city bus to the Greyhound station to catch a ride back home."

"Still not driving?" Theodora asked.

Betty shook her head.

Standing, Theodora said, "I'll drive you to the bus station."

"No thanks. I'll make it." She paused. "Just one thing, why were you following me back at the motel? Why didn't you say hello then?"

Theodora blinked. "What motel? I saw you running through the parking garage. I had just parked my car."

Betty retraced her steps to the city bus stop. As she waited, her mind jumped ahead to the long trip home on the road. Blood thumped in her ears. Her breaths grew shallow. It was just a bus ride, she reminded herself.

She knew the statistics. Tens of thousands of fatalities from car wrecks each year, but only hundreds from bus wrecks. "The odds are in my favor," she said out loud. The city bus came into view. Oh, how she wished she was already home with LB.

The bus stopped. The door opened.

Fear thou not for I am with thee. Betty squared her shoulders and boarded the bus.

Chapter 11
Fast, fast, hearts faint in vain
Floors upend when wisdom gained

Betty propped her elbows on the picnic table. It was Wednesday, the day after her Fort Worth excursion, and she and Flora were eating their sack lunches at the Nest.

The Nest was a picnic area behind the Coop. Large umbrellas shaded picnic tables. Elementary school kids' artwork graced the side of the Coop's building. And strips of lawn, sparingly but sufficiently watered, made a windowpane pattern around and between the picnic tables.

"I'm telling you, Flora, Sylvia's grandfather couldn't have done it." From the nearby strip of grass, sunny heads of dandelions bobbed in the breeze.

Flora held a paper clip dispenser in her hand and was circling it above her lunch, an apple, a bag of corn chips, and a delicious-looking turkey sandwich with bacon, lettuce, and avocado spilling out the sides. And two brownies. "Then why'd he run off?"

Brushing aside her curiosity about the paper clips,

Betty said, "Assuming he isn't already dead and buried somewhere, he could have run off because he witnessed the crime, and he's scared he'll be permanently silence. But that doesn't make sense," she said, arguing with herself. "If he witnessed the murder, he'd run straight to Miller and demand the killer be arrested. Anyway, last week you were convinced Hank killed Sylvia."

Reversing the direction of the paper clip dispenser circles, Flora said, "Have you crossed Hank off your suspect list?"

Flowers for me, birds for her. She is really into birds.

"Yeah, Hank still talks as if she's alive." Betty's eyes followed the paperclips. "If he did kill her, he's an awfully good actor. At seventeen, I don't think he could be such a cool cucumber about it. Besides, I think he's a pretty good kid."

Flora made small circles over her brownies. "You've been talking to Mr. Young again, haven't you?"

"I've been talking to Hank himself. And reading his poems." Betty couldn't stand it anymore. "What in the world are you doing with those paper clips?"

"The paper clips? They don't do diddly squat. It's the magnetic holder. You magnetize your food, then your body can't absorb the magnetized calories."

Betty laid her sandwich down and rubbed her temples. "Flora, please tell me you are *not* that gullible."

Pausing mid circle, Flora said, "Are you saying I'm stupid?"

"No, honey, I just–"

"It worked for Carmine Caskcut."

"Who?"

Flora rolled her eyes. "You know, the star of *Glitter My Eyelashes* on Hulu."

"Of course." Betty's words came out deadpanned.

"You see, Jacqueline said Bartholemew's sister down in Waco said she was watching a Hollywood news show, and it was all about Carmine Caskcut's dramatic weight loss. Well, it was about her divorce and the feud with her co-star and the lobsters living in her swimming pool, but it was about her weight loss, too."

"I see." Another employee passed under the shade of the awning on the way to an empty picnic table. Betty gave him a weak wave.

Laying the paper clip dispenser to the side, Flora picked up the first brownie. "I have to eat the brownies first or else the chocolate will melt in this heat." She took a bite. "Anyway," she said around her mouthful, "if a big time celebrity can lose weight on the magnetism diet, so can I."

"I see," she said again. "Back to the issue at hand, yes, I've crossed Hank off the list. My trip to Fort Worth was a bust, so I hate to say it, but our friend Jacqueline's still on the list. And Bartholemew."

"And Mr. Smith."

"Okay, Mr. Smith, too, even though I can't think of a motive. Of course, there's still Fernando and his temper. According to Wanda, he was angry with his mother for renting the old Sanchez place to the Smiths for such a low price."

Homer Cooter, who also worked at the Coop, stopped at their table. "Hi, ladies!"

His nametag read, *Homer Buffo Cooter*.

"Afternoon, Homer," Betty said.

Flora's mouth was full. She gave him a quick, closed-mouth smile.

"I thought I might find you here," he said to Flora. "Boss lady moved our meeting to four o'clock. I texted you, but your phone is on your desk." He glanced at Betty. "You all can take your time eating lunch."

Flora gave him a thumbs-up.

After Homer went back inside, Betty said, "I never knew his middle name was Buffo. Homer Buffo Cooter, what a name."

Flora nodded then swallowed. "His mother and daddy had a way with names. They didn't pick out names beforehand. They waited until they met the baby, to judge the child's personality. Homer Buffo came home from the hospital with hiccups, which made his mother laugh 'at her little buffoon.'"

"Interesting."

"Word has it Elrod *Snew* Cooter," Flora continued, making a face when she said *Snew,* "cried his first twenty-four hours out of the womb and gummed his mother's nipple so hard it bled. Their youngest, Savannah Honey Cooter—Do you know her, the buck-toothed girl who scoops ice cream at Midtown Creamery?"

"Buck-toothed?" Betty said. "Yes, I know her. She has a *pretty* smile."

"If you say so. Well, she didn't utter a peep and didn't wet her diaper for two weeks."

Betty raised her eyebrows. "Only two weeks?"

"Two weeks is a long time," Flora said with a straight face.

Maybe Flora was that gullible.

Flora broke open her bag of corn chips. "But how are we going to narrow it down to one of the four adults?"

A grasshopper clicked its way through the air, landing on the picnic table.

"I've got it!" Betty said with a snap of her fingers, scaring the grasshopper away. "You are right. All four suspects–Jacqueline, Bartholomew, Mr. Smith, and Fernando–are adults."

"*Suspects,* well look at you, Nancy Drew."

Betty cleared her throat and continued. "Our four suspects are adults, like you said, and as the kids reminded me, only adults read the newspaper. We'll put a notice in *The Tulip Times*, something cryptic only the killer will understand, and lure him or her to the scene of the crime. Only the killer would know where the scene of the crime is."

Flora was busy picking a paper clip out of her corn chips.

Betty popped the last of her tuna sandwich in her mouth and chewed. They'd have to tell Miller what time to be there, too. She swallowed. "How to word the notice…"

"I'm on it, Detective Bell." Flora saluted. "You know I do all the community announcements for the Coop. I'll know whose ear to bend." She counted off on her fingers. "*The Tulip Times*, the Eastland paper, of course, and both Fort Worth major papers. Hmm, maybe Weatherford, too." She checked her watch. "If I hurry," she said, stuffing the remains of her lunch back in her lunchbox, "I can get it done in time for tomorrow's editions."

Betty zombie-walked into the kitchen Thursday morning. Nightmares full of sledgehammers had repeatedly startled her awake and left her with a headache and dry eyes. Her bare feet made dull swishing sounds on the linoleum. She shuffled up next to LB at the coffee pot, kissed him, and poured herself a cup. The steam caressed her face. She inhaled. The aroma was like chocolate without the cloying sweetness. Or the scent of rain in a cup. It smelled like thirty-five years of marriage, hands grasping warm mugs in the winter, and soothing rituals.

"Coffee is proof that God loves us," she said.

They sat down at the kitchen table with *The Tulip Times*. A white saucer with a dried date was waiting for Betty.

"Is this breakfast?" she said, pointing at the little plate.

"It's our coffee date." His eyes sparkled.

Her breath caught. She leaned over and gave him another kiss, her eyes filling. "You don't know how perfect your timing is."

She took a bite of the date and sat back, watching her husband read.

After a minute, LB broke out in a laugh so hard that coffee came out his nose. He pointed at the classified ads. "I found your message to the killer."

"Flora's notice, I can't believe I forgot!" Betty snatched the paper from her husband. In text so big that she could have read it wearing dark glasses at midnight was Flora's notice.

> There once was a person who did bad.
> Please pay or be pinched by a crawdad.
> Tomorrow high noon
> At the house, front room.
> That is the end of my want ad.

On Friday a little before the "high noon" of the notice, Betty and Flora stood at the window in Sylvia's former bedroom. The house didn't smell as bad as when Sylvia's dead body was still in it. Flora was still panting from their climb up the staircase.

"I wonder if Sylvia ever stood here and waited for her friends to arrive," Betty said. "It's a straight shot from this window up the road. You can see a car half a mile away, maybe more."

"She wouldn't have done that," Flora said. "You're the one who told me she was a loner. There weren't any friends to come for a visit."

The windowsill was hip height and broad. Betty put the heels of her hands on the lip of the sill and leaned closer to the glass. "Hey, what's this?" There was a design drawn in the dust.

The two women examined it closer.

"An initial, I think," Flora said. "Is that a letter E?"

Betty looked at it from another angle. "Maybe it's a fishhook." She took a photo, another memento to remember her deceased student. "I imagine Sylvia doodling in the dust as she gazed up the road, maybe watching flocks of blackbirds approach."

"Or watching enemies approach."

"Yeah, or enemies," Betty said. Her throat tightened, and heat bloomed behind her eyes. "She tested me that first day, but even so, I saw the talent in her poem. She was sad or lonely or traumatized and acting out. By the next class, she had softened, and she was heeding the school rules. Since I've been reading her poetry journal, I've seen an even softer side of Sylvia. She enjoyed things like wind on her face and rain knocking on the roof. Edith Wharton fascinated her. She delighted in birds."

Flora looked at her, and for once didn't say anything.

Examining the drawing in the dust again, Betty said, "Maybe she did see her killer approach. This doodle or initials or whatever it is could be a clue. Maybe she started to write the killer's name then gave up and tried to run away instead." She let out a long, shaky breath. "But she didn't make it."

Flora swept her arms wide and turned a circle. "Or this could have been her happy place." Her voice was too bright. "Maybe she enjoyed watching sunsets. The window faces west."

Betty managed a small smile. She could tell Flora was trying to cheer her up.

Checking her watch, Flora said, "It's almost noon. What time did you tell Miller to get here?"

"Me? I didn't tell him anything. You're the one who wrote the notice for the papers."

Flora's eyes grew big. "Uh-oh."

"*Uh-oh* is right. We're in an abandoned, isolated

house, and we're waiting for a killer to arrive." Betty was already dialing Miller's cell when Flora clutched her arm.

"I see a car!"

Betty's mouth went dry. The murderer was coming. Miller's phone rang once, twice.

"Miller."

"Muh," Betty said. Her tongue was stuck to the roof of her mouth and didn't want to cooperate. "The farmhouse," she managed. "The killer is coming." She hung up.

"Why'd you hang up?" Betty had moved to the side of the window, just one eye peeking around the edge. "Don't you know you're supposed to stay on the line?"

"No, I've never called a deputy because a killer was on his way!"

"Or her way."

Crouching down below the sill, Betty popped her head up for a quick look. "It's a white SUV." Her heart sank. Jacqueline drove a white Cadillac.

"Okay, then," Flora said. "Jacqueline drives a white Caddy, and Mr. Smith drives a white Navigator."

It could still be the grandfather, which made Betty feel only slightly better. If it was Mr. Smith, at least she didn't know him personally, but the thought of one family member murdering another... She shook her head. "Let's go downstairs."

Flora had turned pale. "Let's hide until Miller gets here. There's a *murderer* coming."

They could hurry downstairs and run out the back door. Betty stood. No, they couldn't. Flora wouldn't be able to keep up. "Yeah, let's hide."

Flora let out a moan.

"What is it?" Betty asked.

A sudden flood of tears washed over Flora's eyes. "It's a Caddy. It's Jacqueline."

Betty's bowels suddenly felt hot. She took Flora's hand and, walking on shaky feet, led her toward the stairs. "Let's not hide. We know Jacqueline. Let's talk to her, see if she'll turn herself in."

Flora scuffed along behind Betty. "*Talk* to her?" Flora said. She whimpered. "Jesus, oh Jesus."

A siren sounded in the distance. "We'll be okay," Betty said. They descended the stairs. "Miller is close."

As Betty and Flora stepped onto the old porch, still holding hands, Jacqueline climbed out of her car with a sleek duffle bag. It was berry-colored and matched her latest fingernail polish.

Flora dropped Betty's hand and gasped. "Is that a real Tumi bag?" She stepped to the front of the porch.

The deputy's car was in sight now.

Jacqueline scrunched her face. "What are you two doing here? I came to see Sylvia." The sun penetrated the top layers of her big hair and made it glow like a halo.

Betty's hands flew to her face. "Flora, we've made a big mistake." She dropped her hands. "Jacqueline, is that bag full of what I think it is?"

Jacqueline shifted the bag on her shoulder and folded her arms. "Just like I said, she came to Tulip to blackmail me."

"So, you're here to…" Flora said.

The noon heat was putting a sheen on Jacqueline's face. She rolled her eyes. "I guess now you'll know, too, Flora. Sylvia is my daughter."

Betty bit her lip and willed Flora not to let on that she already knew. To Betty's surprise, Flora said, "It's hotter than a pound of lard in a skillet out here. Come on inside where it's shady. We got something to tell you."

Miller turned off his siren and slowed. He was leaning toward the windshield with a puzzled look on his face. Betty gave him a weak wave and a half smile before turning and following the other two women into the house.

Jacqueline stood in the center of the living room, looking around. She clutched her bag and peered down the hallway where a scrap of the deputy's yellow tape lay. "Bless their hearts, they're living in a crime scene. No wonder she wants..." Jacqueline patted the bag.

"No, you don't understand," Betty said. She glanced at the dusty sofa and decided not to ask Jacqueline to sit.

Jacqueline took a step back. "Betty Bell! You mean you, too?" She turned to Flora. "And how much do *you* want, Flora?"

"We've got some bad news, sweetie," Betty said, her voice gentle. She took a step toward Jacqueline. "There won't be any money exchanging hands today. You see–"

"Sylvia's dead!" Flora blurted out.

Jacqueline's arms went slack. The bag slipped off her shoulders. "My baby is..."

"Yes, dear," Betty said just as Miller came in the front door.

Jacqueline's designer bag hit the floor followed by Jacqueline.

Betty lunged for her fallen friend. "She fainted."

She patted Jacqueline's cheek. "Jacqueline?"

Miller's feet were planted wide apart. He had his hand on his holster. "What did you two do to Tulip's favorite cashier?"

With a half shrug, Betty said, "Well, Jacqueline's not the killer."

Miller frowned. "And who said she was?"

A twitch from Jacqueline's sandal-clad feet told Betty the woman was coming to.

"Did you ever notice," Flora said, "how big Jacqueline's feet are?"

Betty and Miller helped Jacqueline sit then stand.

Miller said, "How do you feel, Jacqueline?"

"I've never fainted before." She patted her hair. "Did it mess up my hair?"

Betty rolled her eyes. "I think she's fine, Miller."

"My poor, poor baby," Jacqueline said. She sniffed and blinked rapidly as if trying not to cry though Betty couldn't see a single tear. Then she picked up her designer bag. "Tumi and I will be on our way now."

"Who's Tumi?" Miller asked. "Is that your poor baby?"

"No, my poor baby is dead!"

Miller grabbed the short tufts of hair on either side of his head and tugged. "You ladies are driving me crazy." He cleared his throat. His hand returned to his holster. "Mizz Ivy, are you telling me you are related to Chad Kozlowski?" Miller's authoritative, official tone of voice had surfaced.

Jacqueline's face scrunched up in a puzzled expression.

"Who in tarnation is that?" Flora asked.

Betty looked at the deputy, trying to figure out

what he was saying.

Miller opened the front door and escorted the women onto the porch. "We've notified the next of kin. It'll be in tomorrow's paper. The victim is Chad Kozlowski, a boy from Weatherford."

Betty's feet turned to lead. She was rooted in place. "A boy?" Her vision closed in.

"Yes, the boy, the deceased." Miller's voice echoed inside her head.

Betty tried to swallow. "That means Sylvia is still…" There was a whoosh, then everything went black.

Betty came to with five berry-colored dots swishing back and forth in front of her face and what felt like a splinter digging at her back. "What the heck?" Betty said. She blinked until her vision cleared. "Jacqueline, get your hand out of my face."

Jacqueline quit fanning Betty's face. The cashier was bent over, her hair once again a golden halo in the sun. She stood upright, and the halo disappeared in the shadow of the porch. "She's awake. Get her up, you two."

Flora and Miller each offered Betty a hand. She took them and rose.

"Are you telling me," she said, glaring at Miller, "that all this time I thought my student had her *head bashed in with a sledgehammer*, it was actually someone else?"

Miller's eyes narrowed. "And are you telling me,

Mizz Bell, that you have no idea where Sylvia is?"

Jacqueline shook her manicured finger at Miller. "Are you saying Sylvia killed someone? Oh no, not her. She couldn't possibly be a murderer."

Squinting his eyes at Jacqueline, Miller asked, "How do you know Sylvia so well, Mizz Ivy?"

Jacqueline blinked. Betty glanced at Flora who had sucked in both lips. Was it really necessary for Miller to know that Sylvia was Jacqueline's illegitimate child? Or *supposedly* Jacqueline's child, Betty reminded herself.

"Um," Flora said.

"I–" Jacqueline started.

"Because Jacqueline *knows*, Miller," Betty said. "She was a teenage girl at one time." Betty points at Jacqueline, herself, and Flora in turn. "We all were."

Flora propped her hands on her hips. "Yeah, Miller. We were all teenage girls. Were you?"

"Well, I..." He seemed to have trouble finding the right words. "No, but..." Throwing his palms up in defeat, he yelled, "Get outta here, the lotta you. Go on, *git!*"

Jacqueline took off running. Her steps were awkward with both of her hands wrapped around her bag. Flora shrugged and headed toward her SUV. Betty followed after her best friend.

Chapter 12
*I can't stop looking
At the reflection in the mirror
That can't stop crying*

Flora dropped Betty off at home. She slunk inside with her tail between her legs and headed straight for the bathroom. Her stomach was queasy. Her head hurt. She stared at herself in the mirror.

What were you thinking, that Miller, a professional law enforcement officer, didn't know how to do his job? Her eyes looked hollow, and her face drooped, stretching her wrinkles and exaggerating every one of her fifty-eight years. *And how could you have been so crazy as to think Jacqueline was capable of murder?*

After supper, she sat at her desk with her fingers on the keyboard of her laptop. The deadline for *Of Dust and Daisies* was looming. But tonight, her stanzas were anything but the beauty and potency of the Plains. Her words turned dark. She stumbled over syllables and tripped on rhymes.

Mesquite.
Says Pete.
His cheat.

She abandoned the keyboard and tried writing longhand instead. *Fresh sheet.*

Nothing came out of her pen. She sighed. "Defeat."

Suddenly, two hands clasped her shoulders from behind. She jumped then quickly relaxed. "LB."

He massaged her shoulders. "Give it a rest for tonight. You have all morning tomorrow before you have to teach."

Betty's shoulders softened under his kneading thumbs. "Deadline," she said in explanation.

"After a good night's sleep, you could lock yourself in here and work, and I'll fend off dragons, text messages, and solar panel salespeople."

Her computer screen glared at her, mocking her. The window to the back yard was black with night. "I guess it is time to call it a day." She rose and kissed her sweet husband. He tasted like coffee and mint. He was one of those disgustingly lucky people who could drink coffee all day with no ill effects, the rat. It was just like him to brush his teeth then drink another cup.

When Betty lived with her second set of fosters, the O'Malleys, Mrs. O'Malley liked to relax in a hot bath with a good book. She had a nonslip, rubber mat on the bottom of the old, cast-iron tub. It would have been slippery as butter on ice without it. The O'Malleys were an older couple. At the time, Betty thought they were ancient, great-grandparents perhaps. Turned out they were just late bloomers. In fact, Mrs. O'Malley got pregnant for the first time in her late forties, and when the baby came along, well, it was just too much for the couple to manage a newborn and a teenager, so Betty was shuttled off to her third set of fosters.

Betty thought she could have helped the O'Malleys with the baby. She could have held it and changed its diapers and rocked it to sleep. It was painful to be turned away. Why couldn't she have been a big sister to the baby?

Anyway, Mrs. O'Malley had a blowup, plastic shell-shaped pillow. It was pink, and she used it to cradle her head in the tub. The pillow had suction cups on the backside to keep it in place.

With the realization that Sylvia could be a killer–is that why she and her grandfather disappeared? Betty sank into a blue cloud. It went beyond her struggles to write poetry for *Of Dust and Daisies*. Her energy was zapped. Her thoughts chased each other in circles. She'd have to get her mojo back for tomorrow's class. *I haven't even done the lesson plan.*

But Betty couldn't stop fretting over Sylvia. Was she safe? How could her life carry on if the law was looking for her? Every job application in her future, driver's license, apartment application…

Betty prayed for a brighter future for Sylvia then drew herself a hot bath. She grabbed a book and climbed in. She didn't have a blowup pillow, but she did have a hand towel that she rolled up and propped

behind her neck.
I've become my foster mother, after all
.

Chapter 13

Silently flows red water mid rusty cliffs
Silently flows hymns of awe from parted lips

As planned, Betty spent all Saturday morning with her fanny in her chair and her fingers on her keyboard. Only occasionally did her mind wander, to Mr. Smith or Sylvia–*a moon river waltz with Sylvia.* Betty tapped the delete key then typed the last word over: *forsythia.*

Or sometimes she thought about the deceased boy, Chad. Was he trying to break into a house that he thought was still deserted? Or did he have some kind of connection to Sylvia?

Betty checked her watch. It was almost lunch. She stood and stretched and tracked down LB. He was snoozing on the sofa with her phone on his tummy. She left him a note and slipped out the door.

Evidently, Betty and Flora had the same lunch idea because they ran into one another at The Tulip Grocer. Betty selected two pre-packaged salads to take home, and Flora picked a microwavable meal to take back to the Coop. Betty followed Flora to Jacqueline's checkout stand. *Will Jacqueline forgive us for thinking she was capable of murder?*

Betty stared at the candy offerings while waiting her turn. Nothing looked appealing.

"Betty."

Betty looked at the ceiling, sending a prayer up.

"Betty."

Her hands were getting cold holding the chilled salads.

"Betty!"

Betty jumped. Flora was on the far side of the stand with her frozen lunch in a store bag, and Jacqueline was waving Betty forward.

"You're not going to faint again, are you?" Jacqueline said. "Because we don't want to get your clothes all messy." Her heavily made-up eyes scanned Betty from top to bottom. "Of course, if your style is more *casual*, I guess it doesn't matter."

Welp, Jacqueline forgives us.

Betty handed her the first salad, with ranch dressing the way LB liked it.

Swiping the package, Jacqueline said, "Too bad about that girl. I hope they send her far, far away, not to Bridgeport. Bridgeport is too close."

Betty held her own salad back. "What are you talking about?"

Jacqueline leaned forward, her berry-painted nails too close for comfort. "P-R-I-S-O-N." She stood upright. "Don't you think down in Marlin would be better? The further away that horrid mistake of my youth is the better."

"Jacqueline!" Betty shoved the other salad at her. "She has a name, Sylvia. And we're talking about the poor girl's future."

Jacqueline huffed and bagged the two salads.

"Besides," Betty said, lowering her voice to a whisper, "how do you know the grandfather didn't kill the boy?"

"I know because I had to call Fernando to the front to help the old guy carry his groceries out." She shook her head. "Bless his lumpy, old fingers."

Betty tapped her credit card on the machine then slid it back into her purse.

Splaying her fingers for a nail check, Jacqueline said, "He needed a mani, too. A little buffing and a good trim." She tsk-tsked.

"Yeah, but with an adrenaline surge," Betty said, "could Mr. Smith have handled…?"

Juan's mother appeared behind Betty in the checkout line. There were deep circles under her eyes. She had her baby in a nursing sling, a package of diapers in one hand, and a jar of instant decaffeinated coffee in the other. An oversized purse which probably doubled as a diaper bag hung from her elbow.

Mrs. Smelly wiggled the jar of coffee. "Sin became my tenant. Instant is my penance."

The ghost of LB's freshly ground brew from breakfast taunted Betty's tongue. "Coffee is so good it's almost sinful," Betty said with a laugh. "Maybe I should go to confession, too."

Mrs. Smelly didn't laugh along. In fact, she looked serious about drinking instant for penance, and Betty cringed at the thought of drinking that freeze dried coffee-colored water.

Flora said, "My Mormon neighbor drinks instant. He says it's not real coffee, so he's allowed."

Jacqueline nodded. "We always serve the finest whole bean coffee when Bart's brother is visiting. During the pandemic when everybody was out, we had to serve him instant. He hasn't been back since."

"My late mother drank it," Flora said.

"So did mine," added Jacqueline. "Then again, my parents also drank powdered milk. Times were tough back then."

Flora turned to Mrs. Smelly. "Instant coffee is so bad, Fr. Thomas could use the dried coffee crystals to smear on foreheads for Ash Wednesday."

"It *IS* that bad," Jacqueline said. "It's made from scrapings of restaurant coffee makers, the hard, dried-on stuff."

Mrs. Smelly's baby stirred. She put the diapers, jar of instant coffee, and her oversized bag on the conveyor belt and started swaying. Her little boy fell back asleep. In a lowered voice, Mrs. Smelly said, "When Carmine Caskcut did a TV commercial for Java Dirt instant coffee, they kept having to do retakes because she couldn't keep a straight face."

"Java Dirt is actually pretty good stuff," Flora said. "I use it on my roses to ward off skunks. It works great."

Jacqueline handed Betty her bagged salads. "It's only gonna get worse," she said. "The Tulip Grocer is going to carry a generic brand of instant."

All the women gasped.

Mrs. Smelly crossed herself. "I'm converting to Presbyterian."

Flora said she had to get on back to work and left.

Betty leaned over the checkout stand to whisper to Jacqueline. "Well? With a surge of adrenaline, could he have handled a sledgehammer?" She had never met the man and felt bad for thinking this way, but she wanted him to be the killer rather than young Sylvia with her whole life ahead of her.

The baby stirred again.

"*Darsa prisa,*" Mrs. Smelly muttered.

After flashing an apologetic smile at Juan's mother, Betty said. "I'll hurry. Just a sec." She turned to Jacqueline. "Well?"

Jacqueline pressed the receipt in Betty's hand. "No amount of adrenaline could help that old geezer."

Discouraged, Betty shuffled out the door, the bag of salads in hand. She was halfway across the parking lot when she heard someone call her name.

"Mizz Bell, wait up! Are you frickin' deaf or something?"

Betty turned. Fernando was running after her, his store apron flapping. He waved his fist as if he had something to give her.

"I can't believe you made me run after you," he said when he reached her.

Betty pressed her lips shut so the growl that was in her throat wouldn't escape.

"That Williams lady friend of yours dumped her purse out in the frozen aisle," Fernando said. "Her phone was ringing, and I guess she couldn't find it."

Sounds like Flora.

"She left this behind." He handed Betty a car key.

A standard car key, not a smart fob, with the carmaker's logo worn to a smooth, thumb-shaped divot. An old bread tie acted as the key tag. Flora's spare key. "Thank–"

"Tell that broad to keep track of her stuff."

After a stunned second, Betty gathered her composure. In full Jacqueline-style, she smiled and said, "Thank you for returning the key, Fernando. You're sweeter than a batch of pecan snickerdoodles." She tucked the key into her purse. "Even the lumpy ones with burnt edges."

She spun on her heel before he could respond.

Betty could easily picture the jerk with a sledgehammer. Perhaps Fernando thought Chad was one of the tenants. Where was Fernando when Chad was killed? Of course, it'd help if Betty knew exactly when Chad was killed.

Fernando was able bodied and could handle a sledgehammer. He drove. He made regular trips to Fort Worth for Mr. Stevens. On the other hand, he lived in one of the triplexes on the west side of town. On the opposite side of town, she reminded herself, from the Smiths. He'd have no reason to be at the old farmhouse unless... Unless what? Did he even know Chad? Did he know Sylvia?

Once home, Betty handed LB his salad then went to her computer. As she crunched away on green leaves, cucumbers, and feta cheese, she typed Chad Kozlowski's name along with *Texas* into the browser and held her breath, remembering the oodles of Sylvia Smiths she had found on that search.

A list emerged. Miller had said Chad was from Weatherford, and there was only one that was a good match, Chadwick Jason Kozlowski who was mentioned in a Weatherford news station report:

> LOCAL FAMILY RETURNS HOME TO FIND NEW CAR MISSING
>
> "We took the old, beat-up minivan," Paul Alvarez said. "If I'd known someone was going to break into the garage and steal a car, I would have driven the Mustang and left the rusty minivan at home."
>
> "We have four kids," Thelma Alvarez, Paul Alvarez's wife, explained. "We had to take the minivan."
>
> Sixteen-year-old Chadwick Jason Kozlowski was charged with grand theft auto, fleeing law enforcement with lights and siren active, and operating a motor vehicle without a valid license. The East Weatherford High School cheerleader and honor roll student was turned over to the custody of the TJJD. Additional charges under Penal Code Section 71.02 are pending according to the Parker County District Attorney's spokesperson.

Betty checked the date of the online newspaper article. It was four years ago. So Chad would be twenty now. Or was twenty.

She prayed he knew God before he died.

There was no picture accompanying the article, not that it would help. All Betty saw of the boy were his lower legs. Then again, if she had his picture, maybe she could determine if Sylvia and Chad were connected somehow. Did he have a feather tattoo? Were they both into ornithology?

"How can a kid go from cheerleader and honor roll student to stealing cars?" Betty asked the computer screen. "And what in the world is Section 71.02?"

She typed the Texas penal code number into the search bar and read from the first result. "A person commits...establish, maintain, participates..." *Yada, yada.* "...as a member of a criminal street gang." Betty sat back. The young man who was murdered in Sylvia's house was a gang member.

Icy fingers of fear climbed up her neck. She jabbed the touchpad to close the webpage, grabbed her salad, and went to the kitchen to finish eating.

Betty glanced at the microwave clock. "It was a good salad," she said to LB, rising, "but I have an hour before I need to head for class, so I better make good use of it."

She pulled a clean mug out of the cabinet, but there was no coffee made. As soon as she opened the bag of whole bean arabica, LB appeared at her side.

"I'll be glad to make it," he practically shouted. "You go write."

Her posture went stiff, then she slouched. "I yield to the expert." She stepped to the side. "But I'm going to stay and watch you."

"You know," he said, as he dumped the old coffee grounds, "if Chad was a gang member like you said, the

Smiths are probably hiding. Not from the law, but from Chad's gang. I shouldn't have assumed Sylvia's grandfather was the murderer–you know, back when we thought Sylvia was the murder victim. You were right about that."

"It's in her poetry. They wouldn't hurt each other."

He measured the coffee beans, put them in the grinder, and turned it on. "Ten seconds, Betty," he said over the noise. "Then pick up the grinder and give it two shakes while it's still going. That'll knock loose any beans that are stuck under the blade."

Ten seconds and two shakes. "So precise," she said. She had always just kind of guessed. Maybe that was the difference between their brews.

The grinder whirred to a stop. "Beethoven, *he* was precise. Exactly sixty beans per cup."

When the coffee was done brewing, she made her way back to her computer and opened the *Of Dust and Daisies* document.

But it was harder work now. Legs poking out from rubble, street gangs, drugs, graffiti, desperate parents, mournful parents, car thefts… these visions and more kept interrupting her flow.

A soft, sandy Sunday–
There once was a boy named Chad–

"A soft, sandy Sunday," Betty said in a loud voice to draw her attention back to her work.

A harrumphing sigh, a hound's soporific way–
He was a rebellious lad,
He stole a car,

*Didn't make it too far,
Before the law–*

"Betty?" LB poked his head in the door. He pointed his thumb toward the front of the house. "It's your featherheaded friend. Want me to tell her you're working?"

Betty frowned. *Featherheaded* described Jacqueline, but LB liked Jacqueline and wouldn't call her that.

Flora.

Betty stood and marched over to LB. "Really, LB? She's my best friend."

"And she's making a nuisance of herself out front."

Then Betty heard it. A herd of wild boar, an angry bobcat, a high school cheerleading squad, or Flora. It could have been any of them. Betty went outside barefooted.

"Yoohoo, Betty, over here!"

Flora's Blazer was parked on the street in front of the house, and Flora was standing by the hood, wearing a fushia-and-cerulean tunic and waving her arms. "I see you, Flora." Betty walked gingerly on the hot, concrete driveway. It was supposed to be back up in the triple digits today.

"Aren't you working this weekend? We just saw each other at the grocery store. What are you doing here? Oh, and I have your spare car key."

Flora patted her pants pocket as if searching for her key. "I didn't know I lost it. Anyway, I am working. I just deposited an affidavit at the surveyor's dropbox. I didn't want to call you because you always give your phone to Loony Brain when you're working a deadline."

That was true. Not the "Loony Brain" part but the phone part.

"We've solved the murder!" Flora jumped up and down, and her ample bosom followed shortly behind.

"What?"

Flora rubbed her hands together and grinned. "Chad's murderer." Her voice echoed off the brick house across the street.

"Shh, Flora, keep it down." Betty glanced up and down the street then said in a low voice, "You know who killed him?"

"Well, not exactly, but I know who he is."

"So do I. I found his full name, Chadwick Jason Kozlowski," Betty said. "Stole a car and went for a joy ride. He was sixteen and in a gang."

Rolling up on her toes, Flora said, "That all ya got?"

"Well, yeah." Sweat was starting to roll down her chest. "Hurry up, it's hot."

Flora fanned her face. "Yeah, I'm wilting. Anyway, you know how the Coop publishes those community highlight newsletters?"

Betty nodded.

"I looked back to see if there were any East Weatherford High stories, you know, like kids fixing up the park and raking old folks' lawns and stuff."

Betty nodded again.

"I found him. He and some classmates did an eco-project where they went around neighborhoods and collected old paint. A lot of people just toss out the half empty cans. You're not supposed to do that."

Betty sucked in her lips. What had she done with the remaining quart of Cloudy Snow, the last paint color she had applied to the bedroom walls?

"The kids took all the old paint to the hazardous disposal site."

"So, he was an environmentally conscious teen," Betty said, "as well as a gang member. What of it?"

Another grin slowly spread across Flora's face. "I got his picture."

A rivulet of sweat tickled Betty's neck. "Flora, you rock!"

"It's the same boy as the one in the Polaroid picture."

Betty felt her eyes grow wide. "Sylvia had a picture of Chad, and Chad was killed at Sylvia's house. They had to have known each other."

"Exactly." Flora lifted the hair from her neck and turned so Betty could fan it, a routine the two friends had fallen into over the years.

Betty stood on one foot to let the other cool off. "Sylvia and the blonde girl might know each other, too. If so, the blonde girl might know where the Smiths would go to hide."

Flora dropped her hair and turned around. It was Betty's turn to get the back of her neck fanned.

Betty said over her shoulder, "It'd be better if they turn themselves in rather than law enforcement having to bring them in."

"Agreed. We have to find the blonde girl. Let's go to Weatherford."

"Now?" Betty turned back around and stood on one foot again. She was aware she looked like a middle-aged flamingo.

"Not now, silly, I'm working, and you have class. I'll take Monday off."

Sweat was pooling in Betty's bra. "Sounds good," she said, already returning to the house on burning feet. LB would have to cool off the car and drive her to class today. She waved at Flora without turning around. "I'll let you go now, bye."

Once inside, she leaned against the front door and breathed. *Oh Lord, thank you for air conditioning!*

Class went as best as could be expected. Juan finally noticed Sylvia's absence. "Hey dudes, where's the Goth chick?" And Julie was in top form:

> *If you came down with the flu*
> *And had to live at the zoo*
> *I'd climb in your cage*
> *And make sure you don't have mange*

Chapter 14
Walking corpses, screaming veins
Needle pricks to pause the pain

When Monday morning rolled around, a cold front was blowing in. Betty wanted to get Mama Teach's help before she and Flora headed off to Weatherford. She laced up her shoes and stepped outside into the breeze.

With the wind at her back, she flew south down Main Street in the opposite direction from the Creamery and the Grocer. Turning at Avenue G, she slowed. The wind hit her from the side now, threatening to knock her legs askew and trip her, and the hem of her shorts snapped against her legs. She'd have micro bruises on her thighs by the time she got home.

"Yes, it's hot, but we have prayer conditioning," said the church marquee.

I should have called yesterday to ask if I could come over. But the day had gotten away from Betty, so she was hoping to catch the elderly woman enjoying the morning breeze before the rain closed in.

Mama Teach wasn't on her porch. She was in her

front yard, digging up a dog-rose bush.

Sprinting across Mama Teach's lawn, Betty yelled, "What are you doing?" She came to a stop and picked up the old woman's fallen walker. "You're supposed to be recuperating. You're going to break your hip all over again."

Two cats, both black with white bibs, crouched in the window, watching Mama Teach work.

Mama Teach jammed the point of her shovel into the ground and leaned on the handle. "Going stir-crazy doing nothing. *Rest, Mama Teach.*" Her crackling voice took on a mocking tone. *"Relax, Mama Teach. You should retire, Mama Teach. You've earned it, Mama Teach.* What, you think I earned the right to sit around feeling lazy?"

"Well, I…"

"As long as the good Lord keeps me on this earth, I'm going to keep on doing."

Betty nodded. "Of course, but your hip."

"Meh." She waved away Betty's words. "Just a little achy is all." She pulled the shovel out of the ground then went back to work. "Now, help me move this bush, child."

"Yes ma'am. Want me to shovel?"

"I'll shovel, you get down there and lift the root ball."

Betty knelt and clawed at the bigger stones tangled in the roots while Mama Teach worked the shovel around the other side. The bright pink flower heads nodded in response.

"It's a beautiful bush," Betty said.

Now that Betty was actually at Mama Teach's house and talking to the woman, she didn't know exactly how to broach the subject. It'd sound stalker-creepy if she just said, *I need to find a teenager I've never met before, and I'm not related to her.*

Flora would just pull the dog out from beneath the porch.

Here it goes, Flora. Betty took a big breath and started talking. "Mama Teach, I need to find out about a student who went to East Weatherford High four years ago."

"Interesting. What's the student's name?"

"I don't know. I have her picture, and I have her boyfriend's name and picture."

One of the cats pawed at the window.

The old woman paused mid-shovel, bent over with one hand on the handle and the other on the shaft. She closed one eye, the other eye gazing into the depths of the rose bush.

Betty waited.

Mama Teach neither moved or spoke. Was something wrong?

"Mama Teach?"

No response. Was she breathing?

Both cats pawed at the window.

Was she having a stroke? Betty leapt to her feet. Dread filled her chest. A scream formed in her depths. She opened her mouth to let it out.

"I know just the person," Mama Teach said. She resumed shoveling. "Miss Denver. She teaches ninth and tenth grade math and can talk to a doorknob for five hours straight. Thing is, she can't tell the difference between what she is supposed to talk about and what she isn't. Bless her sweet tea."

Betty dropped to her knees and let out the pent-up

scream as a long, wheezing exhale.

"You got asthma or something, child?"

Waving her off, Betty reached once more for the root ball. She leaned into the bush, getting poked and scratched so she could get both hands on it while Mama Teach pried from the opposite side. They tugged and shoved until the flowery bush released its hold.

Both cats jerked to attention, sitting tall at the window, and a terrible thought rose in Betty's mind. "You're not moving the dog roses because of your cats, are you?"

Scowling, Mama Teach lifted her shovel and swung it at Betty's head. The old woman wasn't fast, so it was easy for Betty to dodge the business end. She scrambled to her feet.

"Why'd you do that, Mama Teach?" Betty said. She brushed her hands. Drops of blood were mixed in with the sandy soil.

"Dog roses because of the cats?" She swung the shovel again, this time at Betty's hip. "You think I don't have any sense?" Her wrinkled eyes narrowed. "You've been spending time with Jacqueline again, haven't you?"

"She's a friend."

"She may be sweet and all, but I have a willow stump with a higher IQ."

"Mama Teach!" Betty put her hands on her hips. "That's not very Christian of you."

"Nevertheless," the old woman said, "I'm not moving my rose bush because of the cats. Hank Young told me it'd grow better on the south side of the house, and he knows everything there is to know about roses. Now c'mon, I've already got the hole dug."

Betty wasn't surprised that Mama Teach knew of Hank's flower expertise. But how many other people knew? Hank really needed to come clean with his parents and Julie before there was some kind of explosive confrontation.

Mama Teach wrapped her gnarled hands around her walker and scooch-stepped, scooch-stepped toward the side yard. She paused and turned her head, her face of wrinkles like a damp linen cloth that'd been wrung out. "Well, hurry up, child."

Betty squatted low to get underneath the thorny part of the bush and lifted the plant by its tangled roots. Her years of running made the lift easy, but she had never had strong arms, and her biceps burned. She wished she could simply sling the prickly thing over her shoulder. She followed after Mama Teach.

As the two women settled the floral bush in its new home, Mama Teach explained that summer classes at East Weatherford let out at noon each day. "You won't see Miss Denver leave the building until about one o'clock. Like I said, she'll be talking to one doorknob or another. Everybody's her friend. Everybody, doorknob species or otherwise."

"How will I recognize her?"

"She'll have hair the color of Jacqueline's nails."

Betty pulled back in disbelief. "Berry hair?"

"No, the color before that."

Picturing the fern-colored fingertips Jacqueline sported the week before last, Betty said, "You can't mean the green–"

"That's exactly what I mean. And she wears a thing on her neck."

"A thing?"

Mama Teach splayed her crooked fingers and pointed them at her neck. "You'll see." She squinted at Betty. "Are you driving yourself?"
"No."

"Still not driving, eh? What happens when your husband passes or Flora's car breaks down?"

"Um, Uber?"

The old lady grunted.

A cloud slid in front of the morning sun. Betty hoped the drive to Weatherford wouldn't be in the rain.

"I'll lend you my pass," Mama Teach said. "It won't get you in the building, but it'll get you through the gate to the teacher's parking lot."

Showered and in her skivvies, Betty stood before the closet, thinking about what to wear. Flora would pick her up in five minutes, so she had to hurry. Her cream-colored silk blouse was her nicest top and would convey a confident and serious demeanor. She slid her arms in the sleeves. The material flowed around her shoulders like opaque water. She was wearing her black bra because it was the only one with padding, and it made her feel like she was wearing a grownup bra rather than a pubescent girl's training bra. Since the blouse was opaque, the bra didn't show through. She selected her chocolate-brown, pleated slacks to finish the outfit. The pants went well with the blouse but still looked casual enough for her to be approachable.

She wore her sneakers. No telling how far she and Flora would have to walk today.

When Flora pulled her SUV onto the interstate, Betty let go of the edge of the seat she'd been clutching and dug an old rosary out of her purse.

"You still have that thing?" Flora asked.

"Keep your eyes on the road."

"We're not Catholic."

"The O'Malleys were. You know, my second set of foster parents." Betty rolled a blue bead between her thumb and forefinger while the Lord's prayer swam in the back of her mind.

Flora nodded. She reached over and patted Betty's thigh. "Don't worry none. I'll drive careful as a whore at a tent revival."

"Flora, the things you say!" Betty moved to the next bead. "Both hands on the wheel, Flora."

Ahead on the freeway, a steel gray cloud bank awaited. As they grew closer, Flora flipped on her lights, and Betty closed her eyes in prayer. Soon, raindrops fell, sharp clicks against the windshield. The sound grew to deafening thumps as if the two women were inside a bass drum.

Betty thought she heard Flora calling out for Jesus. "What is it, Flora?" Betty squeezed her rosary as tight as she squeezed her eyes shut, too scared to look. The car slowed.

"We're okay, Betty," Flora shouted above the rainfall. "Everybody's slowing down. It's impossible to see."

Betty's breath came in hitches. She started to relax.

If they got in a wreck at this speed, it'd only be a minor fender bender. They'd survive. They might drown, but they wouldn't die in a bloody wreck. She opened one eye.

The windshield wipers were moving faster than her eye could follow, and it still looked like a solid sheet of liquid waterfalling on the glass. Red taillights from the car in front of them glowed through the gray environment.

Flora thumped the steering wheel as she took the turnoff. "We're gonna be late."

"It's okay. Mama Teach said Miss Denver is so chatty that she won't even exit the building until about one o'clock."

Four miles later, they turned into the school gates. Flora took Mama Teach's pass and pressed it to the scanner. "It's not going to work in all this rain," she said, but the deluge had backed off to a mere downpour, and the gate rose. Flora's arm was dripping when she rolled her window back up. "It worked, how 'bout that?"

"Park where we can see the doors," Betty said, thankful that they could see more than ten feet in front of them now. "When she exits the building, I'll run out to meet her." Betty turned to the back seat. "Where's your umbrella?"

"I don't have one in the car."

A little noise left Betty's throat. "But these are my best slacks and my nicest blouse."

"Well, I had an umbrella in the car," Flora said with a sheepish grin, "but that windy sleet storm we had last spring tore it all up, and with the drought we've been having, I didn't think it was ever going to rain again."

After they parked, Betty kicked off her sneakers–her only pair of shoes besides her Sunday dress flats–and rolled up her cuffs. It wasn't that her sneakers would get ruined in the rain. Afterall, she had run through plenty of puddles before the drought hit. But her shoes smelled like barbecue-flavored potato chips when they were wet.

They didn't have to wait long before a green-haired woman with an enormous silver choker around her neck exited the building. Her green hair was as big as Jacqueline's, but only on one side. The other side was buzzed short and brunette, probably her natural color. She popped open her umbrella.

"What is that?" Flora said, her gaze trained on the woman.

"That is Miss Denver, and she's going to tell me who the girl is in the photograph." Betty tucked her phone in her pants pocket then pressed her hand tightly over it to keep the rain out.

"Should I drive you up to the curb?"

"It's only one row of parking spaces from here. I'll run fast." She opened the door and dashed barefooted across the asphalt in the fat rain drops. She leapt for the curb. As soon as her foot touched down, the rain stopped as if God had cranked off the faucet.

"Really, Lord? Could you have stopped the rain ten seconds earlier?" Her silk blouse had gone transparent in the rain, and she could see clear through to the little bow at the dip of her bra.

Miss Denver was folding her umbrella.

"Miss Denver!" Betty waved. "May I speak to you a second?"

The green-haired woman looked up and smiled. "Of course. It's good to see you!"

Have we met? As Betty drew closer, she saw the silver choker was more like a hamster cage.

Miss Denver's gaze passed from Betty's head to her bare feet. "You got boss!" she said.

"Is that good?"

Miss Denver threw her head back and laughed. "I love your style."

Betty opened her mouth, intending to explain to the woman that her see-through shirt and bare feet were unplanned, not something she'd done for aesthetics. Then Betty snapped her mouth shut. Afterall, Miss Denver's most prominent fashion accessory was a hamster cage.

Betty pulled her phone out. "I was wondering if you could tell me about this girl. The picture is four years old, I believe. The boy is–"

"Chad Kozlowski." Miss Denver tut-tutted. "He got in a heap of trouble, went to juvie."

And now he got himself killed.

"The girl?"

"Emmie Piper."

Betty was impressed. East Weatherford's enrollment was 2500, and Miss Denver remembered the first and last names of two students from a four-year-old picture.

"She was one of those quiet types," Miss Denver was saying, "who went on hikes in the woods and granola stuff like that. You know all that fuss about Chad's trial?"

Betty nodded even though she didn't know.

"Can you believe it?" Miss Denver said, her eyes

wide as if still shocked by the news.

"I can't believe it," Betty said with a Julie-like gush to her voice in hopes it'd encourage Miss Denver to keep talking.

"No wonder the girl disappeared. I would, too, if a street gang vowed revenge."

"Against..."

"Against Emmie Piper, silly," Miss Denver said. "Of course, no one was allowed in the juvenile courtroom, but Frank's nephew is Principal Wile's grandson, and he said–"

"Principal Wile?"

"No, silly, Principal Wile's grandson said his mother said her father–"

"That would be the principal." Betty raised her eyebrow. "Are you by any chance related to Flora Willams?"

"Is that Frank's ex-wife? Never met her. I heard she was real nice, though, despite the restraining order. Anyway, Principal Wile said–confidentially, of course– that Chad threatened Emmie in the courtroom."

Betty's damp blouse was beginning to itch. She fought to stay still. "Threatened Emmie because..." Why was this turning into one of Flora's serpentine explanations? Did anybody speak plainly anymore?

Ah, to be sitting quietly in the living room with LB. His conversations were a bit geeky, but they were understandable.

"Because Emmie testified against him, of course. She was just a passenger and claimed she didn't know he didn't have permission to drive the car. In fact, she said she was clueless until the police saw them and Chad stepped on the accelerator."

Betty's hand flew to her chest. "They were in a car chase?" Her knees felt like mud. "Did they survive?"

Miss Denver cocked her hip. "How do you think Emmie Piper testified against Chad Kozlowski if they didn't survive the police chase?" She folded her arms, the loop of her umbrella dangling from her wrist. "At what school did you say you teach?"

Stretching herself to her full height, Betty said, "Tulip High."

Relaxing, the green-haired woman said, "Ah, I see. Bless your heart."

Lord, please don't let me slap the bless right out of her heart. "About Emmie, does she still go to East Weatherford, or has she graduated?" A breeze rose, bringing goosebumps to Betty's arms.

"Emmie should have graduated by now, but she disappeared after the trial. She didn't receive any time at juvie, probably in exchange for testifying, but that's just my hypothesis. I heard she moved away to Aledo. But then I heard it wasn't Aledo but Godley, but then I heard it was Godley, and *then* Aledo, then Cisco." She shrugged. "Of course, it's all hearsay, and who am I to spread rumors? She probably just dropped out of school and never left town at all."

Betty's wet, rolled up cuffs chilled her ankles. "Well, thank you for speaking with me, Miss Denver. I'll have to let you go now."

But the fashion-creative woman wasn't done speaking yet. "I heard you all were going to consolidate with Eastland High."

"There was talk, but... I really need to go now." Betty allowed a shiver she'd been suppressing to rise up her spine and clatter her teeth. She thought of something else to ask. "Do you know a student named Sylvia Smith?"

Miss Denver gazed at the gloomy sky as if looking for an answer. "Nope," she said after a moment. Looking back at Betty, she said, "I wonder what it'd be like teaching at a small school. How many subjects do you teach?"

"Just one." Betty made a point of looking past Miss Denver's shoulder at two women exiting the building. "Okay ladies," Betty called out, "I'll let you have Miss Denver now. I've claimed too much of her time already." Betty stepped back.

The women glanced at Betty then at each other.

Miss Denver turned and waved at them. "I'll be right there."

"It was ever so nice chatting with you, Miss Denver," Betty said as she continued to back up. "Let's do it again, soon!"

"Yes, let's! When?"

Betty pretended she hadn't heard as she hustled back to Flora's SUV.

If Chad got out of prison then came after Emmie, and Emmie... what? Ran to Sylvia's house to hide?

"Maybe," Betty said. She opened the car door and climbed in. "Flora, the blonde girl's name is Emmie Piper. We need to locate the Piper residence and find out where Emmie Piper was when Chad was killed." She put her sneakers back on and enjoyed their dry warmth.

"But we don't know when he was killed."

"No, but we have a two-week window, give or take."

~

Betty was grateful for the slow speed limits through town. There were only two Pipers listed on her internet search, and they were headed for the first one. Betty was watching the map app on her phone. "Turn right at the next intersection, Flora."

Flora kept glancing at the rearview mirror. "Betty-y-y," she said, "there's someone following us."

She stomped on the accelerator as they rounded the corner.

Betty screamed.

"I love you, Betty! If the murderer catches us and kills us, I just wanted you to know."

Betty's heart jumped around her chest. She twisted around and looked out the back window. "There's no one there!"

Flora braked. Her gaze flitted to the rearview mirror then the side mirror. "Oh, I guess I was wrong. I could have sworn someone was turning every time we did." She laughed, and her eyes closed.

"Keep your eyes on the darn road, Flora!" Betty tugged her shoulder belt tighter.

They drove the speed limit for another block.

"Slow down, Flora. It should be the second house after we cross...oh." A dark-skinned man was tossing an oversized baseball to a preschool-aged and equally dark-skinned child. "Do you see what I see?" The child missed catching the ball but scooped up some muddy dirt, threw it at dad, then spun in a circle with a big grin on his face. Betty smiled.

"Yup. And it looks like that mom's reading on the porch. We're barking up the wrong Piper tree."

They drove past.

Flora stopped at the next intersection. "Where to

next?"

Betty checked her phone. "The other Piper residence is two miles that way." She pointed to the left.

Flora turned. She kept checking her rearview mirror.

"There's no one back there, Flora. Keep your eyes on the road."

But when they pulled up to a two-story, vintage Foursquare house, and Betty climbed out, it felt like someone was staring at her.

"Nice house," Flora said through the open passenger door, "but it looks abandoned. I'll circle the block."

"Aren't you coming with me?"

Flora rolled her eyes. "You're not very good at this private-eye stuff. Don't you know the getaway car can't park out front, or else it'll draw attention?"

"A getaway car? We're not bank robbers." Leaving her purse in the car, Betty closed the door, expecting Flora to turn off the engine, lock the doors, and follow, but Flora drove away.

Betty huffed then turned toward the house. A sidewalk covered in damp leaves led to the wide front porch steps. Betty picked her way carefully–the leaves were slick–and stopped before the stairs. They reminded her of the old Sanchez farmhouse steps with their warped boards. She tested the first step. It held, so she carefully made her way to the front door.

There was no doorbell. She raised the knocker and gave it a few thumps. It was like hitting concrete the door was so solid. While waiting, Betty noted the intricate cornice brackets and the fancy, turned balusters. But paint curled in flakey strips from the brackets, and the balusters stood cracked and crooked.

Maybe the Pipers were renovating it, like Sylvia and her grandfather had been doing at the Sanchez house.

A movement from the side of the house caught Betty's eye. She gingerly stepped off the warped porch. "Hello? I'm looking for the Pipers." When no one answered, she made her way to the corner. The lawn was patchy, and she stepped on tufts of grass to avoid the post-rain mucky bits.

No one was along the side of the house, but a first-floor window was open. Betty approached. "Hello?" She peered inside and was sad to see the window had been open during the storm. Water puddled on the wood floor beneath the window. From the dead bugs and mess of leaves inside, it looked like the window had been open for some time. She tried to push it shut, but it was stuck.

A rustle sounded behind her. Betty whipped around. A squirrel skittered under the hedge separating the Piper's neglected yard from the neighbor's yard. She laughed at herself. Flora had gotten her all nervous about being followed.

The windowsill was low enough she could easily hike a leg over and slip through. She glanced over her shoulder and across the street. No one was watching unless they were in the wet bushes with the squirrel. *I'll just take a quick look around, see if there are any clues as to where the Pipers moved.* "Or a clue to where Sylvia and her grandfather could be hiding," she added out loud.

She stretched her long legs over the puddle on the

floor and stood. A craftsman-style coffee table hugged the wall. Otherwise, the room was devoid of furniture. Fast food wrappers and some other kind of litter were piled in the corner. She approached the debris.

Plastic and metal bits of something–

Needles! Betty backed away. This was a trap house. Did Chad's gang hang out here? Suddenly it didn't seem so outlandish that someone could be hiding in the bushes, watching her buy or sell drugs.

She scurried backwards, forgetting the puddle in front of the window, and splashed through it. So much for keeping her sneakers dry. She crawled through the window. Landing in the slick mud, her feet slid, but she stayed upright. She hurried to the road. *Please be back, Flora!*

With perfect timing, the blue Blazer approached. Flora slowed and pulled over.

After haphazardly scuffing the mud off her shoes on the curb, Betty climbed in. She dug her rosary out, clutched it to her chest, then sank into the seat.

"You look plumb frayed," Flora said.

"It's scary in there." She let go of the rosary long enough to put on her seat belt. "That's not Emmie Piper's house. At least not anymore. And even if Emmie is involved somehow, it doesn't mean she swung the sledgehammer. Sylvia could still be the murderer–or her grandfather unless he's in as poor health as Jacqueline says–and we still don't know where they're hiding." She let out a sigh even Julie would enby. "This trip was all for naught."

"That's weird," Flora said when they made it to the on-ramp. "It smells like barbecue in here."

~

By the time Flora pulled into Betty's driveway, it was dark, and Betty's hands had gone stiff. She slowly uncurled her achy fingers from around the rosary and returned it to her purse.

"Thanks for getting me home safely. And for putting up with my..." Betty tensed her muscles and made a mock-terrified face in the glow of the dashboard.

"That's what friends are for, hon." LB's figure came into view in the sidelight window. Flora scrunched her face. "And there's Lizard Bottom. I'm outta here!"

Betty rolled her eyes and climbed out of the car.

Chapter 15
A woman scorned, her heart is torn
A love once bright, now just a thorn

The next few days moved along pretty smoothly. Cooler weather followed the rainstorm and raised Betty's spirits. Birds sang, dragonflies buzzed, and foliage greened up. But Sylvia was often in her thoughts, and she spent a lot of time on her knees, praying for the girl's safety.

On Wednesday morning, she finished her draft of *Of Dust and Daisies* and got it sent off to the publisher for edits. Retrieving the notebook with her collection of people-observations, she went about the task of writing human-centered poems.

Lunchtime rolled around, and she joined LB in the kitchen. They were making BLTs with avocado–*BLTAs*, LB called them–when Betty's phone rang. The caller ID said it was Mr. Young, Hank's father.

"Have you seen Hank?" he asked, his voice tight. "He's not answering his phone."

"No," Betty said. "Where have you looked? Have you checked with his girlfriend?"

"He's got the truck, and we don't have more than

that ever since the wife's power steering went out, so I haven't been able to look for him."

Worry took hold of Betty. Her lungs were tight.

"I called the library," Mr. Young said, "and Midtown Creamery and his teammates. That blasted girlfriend of his is already out looking for him."

"Maybe it's time to call Miller." She looked at LB whose brow was creased. "LB and I will help, Mr. Young. We'll go out right now."

Mr. Young quickly thanked her and hung up.

"LB, Hank's missing. He took the Youngs' pickup truck, and his dad is stuck at home worried sick."

He put down the knife he was using to slice the tomato and came to her. "Betty, you're shaking." With his arms tightly wrapped around her, he said, "He'll turn up."

Her breath eased. "I'll go south on foot, and you go fetch Hank's dad and drive around the northern part of Tulip so we don't duplicate our efforts."

"Take your phone."

She nodded and went to grab her sneakers.

Four minutes later, running at a good pace on Main, her head swiveling left and right, she stopped at the barbershop. Betty slammed through the front door, panting. Besides a startled Wanda, there were only two others inside, an elderly man getting his hair cut and a bearded, bald man waiting.

"Sorry!" Betty dashed back out, leapt over the flowerpots framing the entrance, and continued south.

Flowers! She stopped and stared at the flowerpots. *Where would Hank go to see flowers?* She couldn't run all the way out to the botanical gardens in Weatherford, but she could check Miami Flowers.

It was only two blocks and a right hand turn away. She sped down the sidewalk, jay-ran across Main, and turned on Avenue H.

Somewhere between Main Street and the florist, Betty asked herself why she was so frantic. It's not like Hank was her own kid, yet she begged God that the boy was okay.

Her phone was getting slippery in her sweaty hand. She tightened her grip.

Tulip could not have another teenager go missing. Betty could not have another student go missing. She had grown to care for the lot. In rhythm with her run footfall, her feelings pounded the sidewalk.

Sassy, rude, wise-cracking, hormone-infused, phone-addicted, fake-strawberry-smelling, hyper, snarky, cliquish, comical, rough, ridiculous, crude, flawed, zany, unfinished, laughable, entertaining, playful, droll, defective, nervous, ludacris, clownish, sensitive, honest–

She reached Miami Flowers' parking lot and aimed for the entrance.

–volatile, witty, soulful, temperamental, smart, wry, outgassing Doritos, and melodramatic. *God, I love them.*

She yanked open the door and stumbled inside the shop, and the eldest Lee sister staggered backwards, her mouth agape and her eyes wide.

Betty's heartbeat sounded in her ears. She gasped for air, sucking in the rose and lavender aroma of the store. "Please don't have a heart attack, Miss Lee." It wasn't the most polite thing Betty could have said, but she couldn't think straight with worry over Hank. "Have you seen Hank?"

The old lady reached behind her and picked up a gleaming pair of pruning shears then waved them at Betty like a weapon.

Betty stepped back. "Please, he's missing."

Miss Lee sliced the air with the sickle-shaped blades. She looked Betty over from her sweaty head to her jittery feet. Apparently deciding Betty was no threat, Miss lowered the shears and said, "In the greenhouse."

After thanking the old lady, Betty dashed outside then sprinted around back.

The greenhouse, a building shaped like a Quonset hut, extended lengthwise from the shop and was twice as big as the brick storefront. Summer shade cloth covered the top, and a giant box fan hummed near the entrance.

She went inside and called Hank's name, her voice raspy from worry and the effort she had expended running. Through the far, translucent wall, she could see the Youngs' pickup truck parked out back. A skunky smell assaulted her nostrils, not unlike the stench that awful day at the Sanchez house. "Hank!" she called again.

The mammoth teen rose from behind the philodendrons with a watering can in his hand and a puzzled expression on his face. Sunlight filtered through the gaps in the shade cloth and sent golden rays that fell on lilies, freesia, and on Hank's face which had never looked more darling.

She almost laughed with relief, but the stench was growing. Fanning her nose, she asked, "What *is* that smell?"

"The Persian fritillary," he said. His face brightened, and he gestured at a human-sized plant with numerous, puce flowers on sturdy stalks. Waxy, blue-green leaves surrounded the base of the plant.

Betty took a step toward the plant, her feet making crunching noises on the crushed shell that served as the floor of the greenhouse. "Who'd want that in a floral arrangement?"

Hank chuckled. "It's not for arrangements. It's strictly for the greenhouse. The smell fools mice into thinking there's a skunk or some other predator in here."

"Amazing." Returning to the issue at hand, she said, "Your dad is looking for you. You had us all worried."

White blotches appeared on Hank's cheeks, and he staggered. "My dad?" He dropped the watering can.

Betty's gaze focused on the Miami Flowers apron hanging off Hank's big frame.

"You *work* here?" Betty said.

Two cars parked alongside the Young's pickup truck. A horde of figures emerged from the cars, too many in fact for any safe or reasonable amount of people. One of the cars was a red convertible. Julie.

"Please don't tell my dad."

Outside voices penetrated the greenhouse walls.

"Does Julie know?"

Before he could answer, Julie burst through the door with Odessa Lynn, Juan, and most of the cheerleading squad.

"Told ya," Odessa Lynn said. She stuck out her chin, her gaze sliding down her nose and landing on Julie's petite form.

"Yo," Juan said, "Hank done hunted down."

Color crept up Julie's cheeks. "Don't be silly." She swaggered over to her boyfriend and slid her arms around his waist. "I knew he worked here."

Hank's eyes grew wide. A single chuckle escaped his too tight grin. Bridget and Juan exchanged looks, their eyes wide. Odessa Lynn's lower lip slid forward.

"Everybody, now," Betty said, using her teaching voice, "let's let Hank get back to work."

"Of course, Hunk," Julie said. She stood on her toes and puckered her lips. He leaned down and kissed her, another chuckle escaping as he stood back up.

Julie visibly straightened and marched toward the door. A smile painted her face, but her chin trembled. She drove away before the others whispered and muttered their way out the door.

Betty and Hank stared at each other.

"How long have you been working here?" Betty finally asked.

He looked down. "Since the beginning of summer, Monday, Wednesday, Friday mornings."

"Where do your parents think you've been going?" She started to text LB but waited for the boy's answer.

Hank's face turned the color of pink azaleas. "To the library, studying for the SAT." His shoulders sagged. "Dad thinks I've got this big football thing ahead of me."

"And you don't think so?" She cleared the text and concentrated on what Hank was saying.

He shrugged. When his gaze met hers, she saw

sadness there. "I guess I'm built to be a football player," he said. "It's just that..." He spread his arms indicating the beautiful blossoms and greenery surrounding them.

Betty desperately wanted to hug the boy, tell him it'd be okay, that his floral interests were both impressive and worthwhile. But it'd be inappropriate. Instead, she pressed her hand against her melting heart and said, "I'm not a parent, Hank, but it seems to me a parent's love–your dad's love–is so strong that his desire for you to be a happy, productive member of society trumps any vicariously lived football dreams he may harbor."

Hank scrunched his face. "What?"

"Your dad loves you," she said flatly. "Do you want to text him and tell him where you are, or should I?"

Hank looked from the lilies to the fiddle leafs as if seeking his answer. "I'll do it." He puffed his chest out. "I'm eighteen now, I can have a man-to-man talk with my own dad."

Betty nodded and left the greenhouse.

On her way home, she said a prayer for Julie whose melodramatic heart must be broken.

The next morning at the breakfast table, LB rushed through the paper and his scrambled eggs.

"Is this the day you're supposed to go to Abilene?" Betty asked.

"Yeah."

"Will you be back in time for dinner?"
"Yeah."

Such simple answers with exactly the information she needed. She ran her hand over his cheek and jaw. He had shaved, but not too closely. Sandpaper whiskers tugged at her fingers.

"What are you doing?" he asked.

She smiled. "Just loving on you, *Elll-Beee*." She drew out the letters, her voice turning husky.

He rose and kissed her on the lips, dousing her with his coffee and soap scent. "Gotta go, but hold that thought for tonight." He grabbed his keys and left.

Betty went for a run, showered, then grabbed her shoes. She'd only be gone for a few minutes, so she skipped the socks. Just a quick trip to the grocery store before the morning grew too hot. When she rounded the edge of the house and started for the backyard, she heard a car speed up out front, spinning its wheels with a squeal.

Betty marched to the front of the house and peered down the street. If it was one of the kids from class, she'd have to have a talk with him or her. All she caught was a glimpse of a white, rear fender, a sedan speeding around the corner.

She turned around.

While walking along the fence next to Petrol Pete's, she made a mental shopping list. Granola, berries…

She turned onto the sidewalk, and an uneasiness seized her. Picking up her pace, she glanced over her shoulder, but there was no one.

Why does this keep happening?

Another tire squeal cut through the buzzing of the

morning grasshoppers. Ahead at a corner stop sign, Miller's car with the dented fender was idling. Her tension eased. Glancing behind her once more to make sure no one was following, she gave him a little *sorry* gesture as she jaywalked across Main, but because of the glare on the windshield, she couldn't make out his face and thus couldn't tell if he was peeved or not.

Once inside the store, Betty grabbed a buggy and headed for the dairy aisle to get a big tub of plain yogurt. Yogurt with granola and blueberries was not LB's favorite breakfast, but she liked it, so she thought she'd take advantage of his absence and indulge.

Rounding the end of the aisle, she caught a figure in the corner of her eye. She backed up. No one was there. Was there someone hiding at the far end of the aisle? She retraced her path and peeked around the aisle. No one was there.

I'm just on edge because I thought someone was following me on the street. She chuckled and teased herself that she only thought someone was following her on the street because she thought someone was following her in Weatherford.

And in Fort Worth. Her chuckle ended abruptly.

She pushed her buggy to the cereal aisle and looked out the front windows for unfamiliar cars or strangers lurking and was relieved to see Deputy Miller's cruiser out there. He must be somewhere in the store.

Her nerves settled.

She plucked a bag of generic granola. Footsteps sprinted by on the other side of the shelves.

She shoved her cart forward past the oatmeal, syrup, and raisins. She spun around the end of the aisle and dodged a startled Juan crouched over the display of sale diapers.

Halfway through canned goods, she risked a glance. Behind her, the aisle was empty.

"I'm losing my mind," she said to the canned corn. She pictured grasshoppers blissfully nibbling on stalks of corn and forced her breathing back to normal.

After a swing through the produce section to pick up blueberries, she headed to Jacqueline's checkout stand, relieved to see a familiar, if overly made-up, face.

Deputy Miller came out of nowhere and inserted himself between Betty and the credit card machine. His breath whistled across his teeth.

"I'm so glad to see you, Miller." She smiled for the first time since she left the house. "I have the feeling someone's been following me."

"Yes," he said with a huff. "Me! I tried to catch you at the house, but you took off on those blasted gazelle legs of yours." His gaze scanned the other customers in line behind Betty: Juan with a package of diapers under his arm. A little kid with a suspicious amount of chocolate on his mouth and no parent in sight. And Bill Ramsbottom.

Deputy Miller cleared his throat. "Mizz Bell, I'd like to speak with you over at the station." His brow tensed.

"Is LB okay?" Her mind automatically pictured his car, crumpled on the interstate. When Deputy Miller didn't respond right away, her knees weakened. "LB!" she wailed. She started sinking to the floor.

Deputy Miller jumped forward and grabbed her upper arm.

She dropped her yogurt. It splattered in a glorious globe of white, like a liquid dandelion. *What a strange thing for me to think at a time like this.* She shook the dandelion thought from her head.

"He's fine, Betty, he's fine!" Miller said. His grip was so tight that the pain brought Betty back to her senses.

Jacqueline lifted the handset to the overhead speaker and pushed the call button with a teal-tipped (the berry was gone, Betty noted) finger. "Clean up at checkout, Fernando. Thirty-two-ounce yogurt, full fat."

Betty was nodding at Miller, relief flooding through her. "I'll just run and grab another yogurt and quit holding up the line."

He didn't let go of her arm. "Leave your groceries, Mizz Bell."

Still with the *Mizz Bell.* "Why? What's going on?"

Fernando arrived with cleaning supplies in hand.

Leaning in, with a lower voice, Miller said, "The station."

"Lord, have mercy," Jacqueline said in a voice that was way, way too loud. "Betty Bell is under arrest for the murder of that Weatherford boy."

"Jacqueline," Betty said through clenched teeth, "your finger is still on the speaker button!"

"Yo, burst the bubble," Juan said. "Teach in trouble."

Smiling best she could while her armpits exploded in sweat, Betty said to Juan and the other two customers in line, "I'm sure we're just going to have a little chat."

But Bill took a step back.

And Fernando made his hand into the shape of a pistol and aimed it at Betty. *Bang*, he mouthed.

Chapter 16
Heat that spreads from heel to toe,
A burning sole, a burning soul.

Betty waited alone in the beige-clad interrogation room, its windowless walls inching toward her. Deputy Miller had escorted her to the station and into the little room then asked for her phone, purse, and shoes. Her feet were getting cold on the industrial tile floor. She should have worn socks after all.

There were two folding chairs and a hefty table. A pad of paper sat on top of the table. Is that where she was supposed to write her confession?

"Confess what?" she joked. Her voice bounced off the cinder block walls. It was all a misunderstanding.

She waited.

Was this an intimidation tactic? On television, the cops sometimes left the suspect alone to get nervous while they questioned the suspect's accomplice. Except Betty was not a suspect, and she didn't have an accomplice.

Well, there was Flora, but the two of them didn't

do anything.

We found the body.

"That's not a crime," she said in response to her own thought.

Betty tapped her foot. She counted the lines on the pad of paper and the tiles on the floor and the number of hangnails on her left hand. Finally, Miller came back carrying a Bankers Box. He didn't make eye contact.

He took a seat in the chair opposite Betty, and then pulled two photographs from the box and pushed them toward Betty.

The first photograph showed Betty at Emmie Piper's abandoned house. Betty was crouched and rounding the corner of the house. She looked like a terrible excuse for a cat burglar. The second photograph showed her climbing either in or out of the window.

"I didn't steal anything," she said. "And I definitely did *not* buy, sell, or touch any drugs."

"And this." He placed a third picture in front of Betty. Her footprints where she had landed in the mud outside the window. Someone had placed a brick next to the prints, probably for size comparison.

Betty shook her head. "You didn't have to take my shoes. I would have told you those are my footprints."

"What were you doing at the former hangout of Jane Eyre?"

"I don't know anyone named Jane."

Miller returned the photographs to the box. "Jane Eyre was Chad Kozlowski's gang."

"It's the name of a classic novel, too."

"Yeah, well, I guess they were educated." He clicked his pen and poised it over the pad of paper.

"*Was* Chad's gang? They *were* educated?" Betty

closed her eyes and tapped her temple.

"Mizz Bell–"

Her eyes popped open. "Do you mean the gang–Chad Kozlowski's Jane Eyre gang–doesn't exist anymore? Was that their hangout before or after Emmie Piper lived there?"

Miller's eyes grew wide. "How–"

"It doesn't matter either way," Betty said, dismissing her own question. "Emmie knew Chad. Emmie testified against him. Emmie and her family left town." Betty sat bolt upright. "That symbol we found on Sylvia's windowsill. It wasn't a fishhook. It was the letters J-E squished together, Jane Eyre!"

"On Sylvia's windowsill? Betty!" Miller's face turned red, all professionalism lost. "This is a *murder* investigation. What were you doing in the girl's–in Miss Smith's room?"

"That was the day Flora and I still thought Sylvia was the victim, when you and Jacqueline came to the house. Anyway, it was written in the dust. You can see clear down the road from that window, so Flora and I think that's where Sylvia watched for someone to approach."

"Interesting." The color returned to normal in the deputy's cheeks. "Continue."

"Well obviously Sylvia saw the now-dead Chad coming because she drew J-E in the dust." Betty smirked. "If I had my phone, I'd show you."

With a harrumph, Miller pulled Betty's phone out of the box and handed it to her. "Show me."

Betty scrolled through the photos until she landed on the right one. "See? It's a J-E squished together."

"Will you text that to me, Mizz Bell?" He was

using his deputy voice again.

She complied, then he took her phone back and put it in the box.

"Now, Mizz Bell, back to the reason you were snooping around the gang's former headquarters."

"Do you know where Emmie is?" she asked. The air conditioner kicked on, and Betty folded her legs beneath her, tucking her cold feet under her bottom. "And who took the pictures of me at the house?" She gasped. "I was right! Someone *was* spying on me in Weatherford. Was it you? And how about Fort Worth?"

"Fort Worth, too?" Miller dragged a palm over his face, pulling his aging skin downward as he did. His eyes looked like the drooping eyes of a hound dog.

"Did you take the pictures, Miller? You can't really think I had anything to do with Chad's death. C'mon, Miller, you've known me for thirty years, and LB since you babysat him as a kid. I'm not a murderer, and LB wouldn't marry a murderer!"

Miller slumped back in his chair. "You've obviously caught the attention of someone else," he said, his official tone gone and his longtime-friend voice back. "Look, I know and love you and LB like you were my own siblings, but if this case comes before the court, the prosecutor has to show we exhausted other possibilities before charging the suspect."

Betty nodded. He didn't actually suspect her. He was just doing his job.

"Let's try another tactic." He consulted his folder. "Where were you on July first at four-thirty-four in the afternoon?"

"Is that the time of death? How'd you narrow it down to the exact time?"

Miller's gaze scanned the ceiling as if he was deciding something. "Say a cell phone suddenly got destroyed. It was tossed from a cliff, for example."

"Or crushed by a sledgehammer," Betty said. She saw where this was going.

"The service provider can determine the exact time when the cell phone stopped working."

Betty smiled. "I do know where I was. I'd been working all afternoon on the narrative poems section of *Of Dust and Daisies,* and thought it was time for a break. It was the first day of cheer camp and football camp. I walked over to Midtown Creamery, but the camps had just let out, so the place was crowded with teens. Darlene, Hank and Juan, Bridget… most of my class plus half the rest of the teenagers in Tulip saw me there."

"Football's a big thing."

"Cheerleading, too."

Miller frowned. "What about Sylvia Smith? Was she there?"

Shaking her head, Betty said, "No, but she could have been lost in the crowd." A pang of guilt stabbed Betty in the gut. She knew darn well Sylvia wasn't there. The girl wouldn't have been hanging out with football players and cheerleaders. "At any rate, I didn't stay. It was so crowded I went to The Tulip Grocer instead and got a pint of Blue Bell."

"Alrighty, then." Miller pushed his chair back and stood up. "Thanks, Betty." He dug her purse out of the box and gave it and her phone back. "I gotta keep your shoes until the case is closed."

Rats, she'd have to get new running shoes.

"I'll drive you home."

Unfolding her legs, she rose to her feet. "I don't want you to drive me home. Juan already saw me get *arrested.*" She put the word in air quotes. "Thanks, but I don't need any other students seeing me in the back of a deputy's cruiser. I'll call LB."

He nodded. "Hey, if someone starts following you again, or if something else turns up, call me." He placed his hand on Betty's forearm. "I'm investigating a *murder.*"

Once outside the station, Betty remembered LB was out of town. No problem, she'd call Flora instead.

What was once a pleasant morning had morphed. The brutal sun had seared the air and turned the concrete to a hot griddle. Betty backed up into the shade against the building where it was cooler for her bare feet. She dialed the electric co-op.

"Flora's not here, Mizz Bell." It was Homer Cooter. "She and the boss lady took the truck out to run the poles, you know, inspect the line."

"Thank you, Homer." Betty hung up. Ugh, she'd have to take Miller up on his offer to give her a ride home.

Before she could go back inside, Miller and Deputy Floyd came barging through the station doors. Floyd hopped the handrail adjacent to the steps and sprinted to his car while Miller took the stairs one at a time and talked with a strained voice into his radio. *Armed* and *bridge* was all she could make out. Betty said a prayer that no one would get hurt. The two patrol cars sped away, lights flashing and sirens blaring.

"Uber it is." She pulled out her phone.

A moment later the Uber notification pinged. *No Cars Available.* Cletus must be at the hospital.

Betty tucked the phone into her purse.

It was only a mile and a half to the house. She pulled her shoulders back and descended the short stairway to the sidewalk, sliding her palm along the handrail that Larry had hopped. She snatched her hand away. The handrail was hot. The sun pressing on her shoulders was hot. The concrete abrading her feet was hot.

She walked as if nothing was wrong. The worst thing that could happen now is for a student to see her desperately fleeing the deputy station. But when she came to the stop sign on Main, she couldn't help but sprint across the street. Its newly resurfaced asphalt was soaking in the heat of the sun and had become hot enough to roast ants.

On the far side, Betty stayed on the paler and cooler concrete sidewalks and aimed for her turn at Petrol Pete's.

Her phone rang. Betty dug it out of her purse. Adhira was calling.

"Hello," Betty said, trying to sound cheerful though her hot feet were making it difficult.

"Any people-oriented poems yet?" Adhira said instead of a greeting.

Betty stepped over a stray nail. "Maybe one about a woman with bloody feet." She went back and picked up the nail and dropped it into her purse. No use in anyone else stepping on it.

"What?"

"Never mind, I'm working on it."

There was a pause.

"Frankly, Betty, you sound like you're in pain. I don't care if it's a headache or your arthritic fingers. Don't be a hero. Just take an Advil and get back to work."

"I don't have arthritis." She flexed her fingers as if Adhira could see. But it didn't matter, the woman had hung up.

Betty had to pass in front of The Tulip Grocer, but at least she'd be on the other side of the street. If Jacqueline saw her walking barefoot, there's no telling what she might assume.

By the time she made it to Petrol Pete's, her feet burned so much she wouldn't have been surprised if they were blistered. She took a quick peek. They were bright red, and the ball of one foot was scraped and bleeding, but no blisters.

She continued.

Seeing the fence where she'd turn brought a sigh of relief. Shade. She jogged the last few yards to the fence and hooked a left. The only thing she had to worry about here was broken glass. She kept her head down.

Finally, on the gravel utility easement approaching the back of her house, she broke into a full run and leapt for the lawn. The grass felt cool. A wasp or even a scorpion might get her, but at least her feet were cooling off.

She rounded the corner of the house and saw Bridget lying in the shade of the front porch, still as death.

"Bridget!" Betty forgot all about her painful feet and knelt by the teen. She shook the girl's shoulders and yelled her name again.

"What's your prob, Miss Bell?" the girl said, sitting up. She yawned, stretching the freckles on her face. Her eyes were puffy as if she'd been crying. But she looked at Betty's feet, and a grin crossed her face. "Hey, you really were arrested." Her expression grew serious, and she gave Betty a knowing nod. "I heard they took people's shoes away in prison."

Betty stood up and glared at the girl. "No, I was *not* arrested."

"Juan says you were."

"It was a misunderstanding," Betty said, a pain growing behind her brow. "Now, what were you doing sleeping on my front stoop in the middle of the day? I thought you were dead!"

Bridget pulled her heels in and sat cross-legged. "Yeah, the dead body thing happens a lot at your house."

"Once, Bridget. It happened once, to poor Ben Higgins, and I had nothing to do with it. Apparently, he was wandering around in the ice storm."

"Wandering around in the ice storm? He had Down syndrome. It's not like he was crazy."

"Anyway," Betty said, "the next morning Miller found him in our back yard, under our pecan tree to be exact. The poor man was dead."

Bridget plopped back against the brick wall. "I

wish I was." Her face contorted, and tears streamed from her eyes.

"Oh, honey!" Betty sat on the concrete next to the girl. "What is it? What's wrong?"

"I'm pregnant."

A big lump formed in Betty's throat, and she tried to swallow it. How many times had she wanted to say those words to LB, and was never able to?

"How far along?"

"Four months."

Betty moved closer and put an arm around the miserable girl. The girl was so flat-bellied she disappeared everytime she turned sideways. "I don't think you're actually pregnant, honey. It's probably stress. Cheer camp, being sent to a summer enrichment class to keep you out of trouble..."

"Duh," Bridget said, wiping her tears. "That's why the school counselor recommended your class, so I wouldn't do anything else stupid."

"Oh."

Betty had heard that the school first asked Tulip High's only math teacher to teach a summer class, but he declined. She was grateful now that Miller had recommended her. Imagining grumpy Mr. Stellars dealing with a pregnant, upset Bridget made Betty cringe. He was so ornery he could start a fight in an empty house.

"My life is over," Bridget said. "No more cheerleading. No more graduation. No more Juan."

Betty gave the girl's foot a pat. "I don't think they can kick you off the squad because you're pregnant. But you're a flyer, right?" The tiny, most petite cheerleaders like Bridget and Julie were the ones who got tossed in the air. "Your coach will probably assign you a different spot."

Bridget sniffed. "No, I *quit* the team. The way we get injured all the time, I don't need to risk injuring my baby."

Betty blinked. "Is that you speaking?" Betty wondered if an adult in her life had put such words in her mouth.

Looking left and right, Bridget said, "I don't see anyone else talking."

They sat in silence for a while. The oak tree had revived since the rain, its leaves growing broader, thicker. A songbird hid in the foliage and sang a melancholy song. The air condenser at the side of the house hummed.

"Why are you here, Bridget?"

"I did the stupidest thing in the world, and I know it and wish it never happened, but my parents and Meemaw..." She hung her head. "I'm tired of getting yelled at."

It was not Betty's place to tell the girl what to do. "I really wanted to be a mother," she said instead, "but it wasn't meant to be, and it's still something that haunts me." Hollowness filled her chest.

"Oh, my gawd, Mrs. Bell, you're old as dirt. You can't adopt my baby!"

Then again, she and LB had avoided the teen years.

Betty sucked in her cheeks and looked at the girl. "What I meant was, *young* couples who want to be parents but can't conceive hurt inside. It feels like thousands of needles right here." She pressed her palms against her tummy and felt the needles now, even after all this time.

"Weird."

"I assume your friends know. They love you. They'll–"

Bridget rolled her eyes.

"Are you seeing an obstetrician?"

She nodded.

"Why don't you think you'll graduate?"

She shrugged and stared at a grasshopper who had landed next to her feet.

"Does Juan know?"

A fresh flood of tears cascaded down Bridget's cheeks. "No. I'm afraid to tell him. He's so Catholic."

"He's so what?"

"His whole family is super religious and has crucifixes on the walls. They even pray before dinner."

"Imagine that." Betty struggled to keep the sarcasm out of her voice. The air condenser cut off, and a sound wave of cicadas began. When the insects had crescendoed then waned, she said, "Life is forcing you to grow up fast. Part of being in a grownup relationship is being honest with one another. I think you should tell Juan. If he's the godly young man you say he is, then he understands repentance and forgiveness."

Bridget closed her eyes and sat quietly. Was she praying? She opened her eyes, wiped a fresh tear off her cheek, and stood. "I guess I'll go now."

Betty rose, too. "Do you have a way to get home? I don't have a car."

"I'll walk," the girl said with a shrug. "You're not the only one in Tulip who doesn't drive. Besides, it's not far. I live in the apartments on the other side of the grocery store."

"Take the shortcut along Petrol Pete's fence." She gave Bridget a drink of ice water then sent her on her way.

As Betty watched the girl recede in the distance, Betty's heart grew heavy and threatened to fall into the vacuum of her empty womb.

What timing is this? New life within
A child herself, my jealousy is sin.
I bow my head, concede His perfect plan,
He comforts me with His divine hand.

Chapter 17

Rich laughter amplified mine,
Sweet fruit of a tender vine.
'Til betrayal crouched in shadows
Devoured all. A barren twine.

After showering deputy station nerves and the afternoon heat from her body, Betty got dressed. She needed to find out who was spying on her at the Pipers' former residence. Did it have anything to do with Chad's murder?

LB still wasn't home, so she messaged Uber. She hoped Cletus was available now.

He was. The app's map showed his arrival in two minutes. Deputy Miller had her only pair of sneakers, so she grabbed her church shoes.

But she couldn't fit her scraped, burned, and swollen feet into the leather flats. She checked the app. One minute.

The only thing she could think to do was put on two pairs of bulky socks and LB's walking shoes. She felt like a clown in his size 12 sneakers, but it was better than going barefoot. She opened the front door just as Cletus arrived in his Prius.

"You have some kind of poem thing going on in Weatherford, Mizz Bell?" he asked when she climbed in.

She pulled her seat belt tight. "I just want to figure out something." To know someone had been spying on her left her feeling exposed, vulnerable. Could she find any clues as to who it was?

Cletus accelerated, and Betty's heart rate accelerated. To keep her hands from shaking, she sat on them.

Cletus stopped at the Highway 6 intersection, and his hybrid engine automatically shut off as it always did to save gas. In the quiet, Betty relaxed, until a Ram 1500 stopped catercorner across the intersection. Cletus's car felt like a Hotwheels to Betty, and the pickup truck looked like a steamroller.

"I'll be just a moment, Cletus," Betty said when she climbed out of his car in front of the Pipers' former home. "Can I have a ride back?"

"Yes, ma'am." He slouched back in his seat and pulled out his phone.

Betty flopped along the sidewalk in LB's shoes, passing the abandoned house and turning at the hedgerow along the edge of the property. Whoever took those pictures had to be hiding in the wet bushes that day, or else Betty would have seen him or her.

Staying close to the hedge, she crept forward until she came across a gap in the foliage. Remembering the photographs that Miller had showed her, she assessed the view. "Not here, not yet," she muttered. She advanced to the next gap. She smiled and waved at the neighbor's house, so she'd look like an innocent, middle-aged woman instead of a dognapper or something. It wouldn't do to get hauled off by law enforcement twice in one day.

Betty crouched and looked through the gap. Yes, this was the right angle. Why had someone been spying on her? And who was it? Was it the same person who sent the postcard?

Checking for footprints in the dried mud, Betty found a sizable, clear print, some kind of sneaker. It could be a big teen's print, a large woman's, or a not-too-big man's. The print was facing the street. The photographer as he or she left the scene, or the homeowner walking the perimeter of the yard?

A glossy trinket caught Betty's eye. She bent down. It was a berry-colored, acrylic nail.

Betty pocketed the nail and stomped back to the car.

"Take me home," she said as she climbed in the car and slammed the door.

If Betty thought she was fit to be tied in Weatherford, it was nothing compared to how she felt by the time Cletus took the I-20 exit leading to Tulip. Betty was seeing red.

But maybe it was the lowering sun in the west. Or the way she had stopped breathing every time Cletus passed another semi. There were a lot of semis on Interstate 20.

She checked her watch. "Just drop me off at the grocery store, instead, please."

Jacqueline must have seen Betty approaching the entry because when Betty burst through the front doors with her feet flopping around in LB's shoes, Jacqueline's eyes were already pooled with tears.

"How could you?" Betty hissed.

Jacqueline's hands were visibly shaking. Her lower lip quivered. Her mascara ran, then so did she.

Betty took chase.

She lost the first oversized shoe in canned goods and the second in dairy. Jacqueline banged through the door leading into the stockroom, and Betty followed. She caught her by the third row of shelves, wrapping both arms around the cashier's waist and took her down.

Even Hank would be impressed with that tackle.

They landed on a pile of flattened cardboard.

Betty rolled the Barbie-shaped woman to her back and straddled her. "I've got something for you, *Jacqueline*." She said her friend's name with venom. Betty fished in her pocket.

Just then, Fernando came through the plastic strip curtain hanging over the loading dock entrance.

Jacqueline arched her back and wailed.

"Oh, hey," he said, stopping short. "The chicks be gettin' it on. Better hurry. Mr. Stevens will be back in, like, five minutes." He did a one-eighty then laughed his way back through the strip curtain.

"No, it's not what it looks like!" yelled Betty, but he was already gone. She looked down again at

Jacqueline and brandished the acrylic nail. "Are you *missing* something, Jacqueline?"

Jacqueline quit struggling and wept silently.

Betty climbed off Jacqueline and stood up. "Why were you following me?" She placed one bare foot on Jacqueline's chest to hold her in place. *Good heavens, her enhanced breasts felt like unripe cantaloupes.* "Why did you take pictures of me at the Piper house?"

"Betty–"

"Why did you give them to Miller and make me a suspect?"

"We've been friends a long time, Betty, and–"

"You don't *betray* friends! Why did you tell one of my students and the whole world over the intercom that I was getting arrested for the murder of Chad Kozlowski?"

The "whole world" was overkill, Betty knew, but if she was going to pitch a fit, she'd pitch a good one. Betty took her foot off Jacqueline, stepped back, and crossed her arms.

Jacqueline rose to her elbows, looking up at Betty. "I thought maybe Julie…" She broke into a sob. It was such an ugly cry that Betty knew the tucked and trimmed, lifted and dyed, painted and fluffed woman wasn't crying crocodile tears.

Betty huffed. "Do you mean to tell me you thought your peppy, little cheerleader killed a twenty-year-old, hardened criminal?"

Jacqueline nodded. She sat up and wept into her hands. "You don't know how…" She wiped her bare arm across her nose, smearing foundation, concealer, and liquified mascara across her face. "It's really bad at home."

Looking around for a tissue or a paper towel, Betty spotted shop rags on Mr. Stevens' desk, a low, wide metal monstrosity squatting against the far wall where he did payroll and invoices. She retrieved a rag then reached down to dab Jacqueline's face. Betty resisted the urge to stuff the rag down the woman's throat.

Jacqueline looked up at Betty through a river of tears. Snot dripped from her nose.

Betty swallowed hard and fought the compassion bubbling up within her. She snarled, but it was fake.

"Oh crap, Jacqueline. You framed me to protect your daughter, didn't you?" The needles in her gut were stirring.

"Can I stand up?"

Betty reached her hand down to help her friend up. "Relax, Jacqueline. Julie has an alibi. The cheer squad and at least half the football team went to Midtown Creamery the day Chad was killed." Something niggled at Betty's brain, but she couldn't figure out what and ignored it.

"Glory be," Jacqueline said, her words gushing with emotion. "Then everything's going to be okay between us, isn't it, dear?" She checked her nails and patted her hair. Her tears had stopped.

Betty did her best to keep glaring, but it didn't work. "I understand why you did it."

Smoothing her store apron and brushing off her fanny, Jacqueline said, "Now be a dear and go fetch my purse from my checkout stand. I need to powder my nose."

Unbelievable. Betty did as requested and hastened–still in LB's socks–to Jacqueline's stand. It was the least she could do after clobbering the woman though she still had the urge to dump pancake syrup on her big hair or tomato juice down her shirt.

"Where are your shoes, ma'am?" a man in overalls and a sweat-stained hat asked. He was standing in the backed-up line to check out. There was an odor of cow manure coming from his direction.

"Where's Jacqueline?" a young woman asked.

"We should complain to Mr. Stevens," yet another shopper said.

A little boy pointed out the front window. "There he is!"

The diminutive man was sliding out of the driver's seat of his pristine Ford F-450. He landed with such speed from his controlled fall that dust rose from the asphalt and pooled around his boots.

Betty had to hurry so Jacqueline wouldn't get in trouble, especially if Mr. Stevens asked Fernando about it.

"Jacqueline will be right back, everybody," she called over her shoulder as she ran toward the back.

Betty burst into the back room and shoved Jacqueline's purse at her. "Be quick, your boss just arrived."

Jacqueline scurried into the employee's bathroom while Betty eyed the big, metal desk. What if Fernando's timecard from July first was in the desk?

She sidled over to the desk, hesitated, then listened for any commotion from out front that would indicate Mr. Stevens had entered the store. Silence. She slid open the center drawer.

Pens and paper clips. *Just one more drawer, and I'll leave.*

She slid the top left-hand drawer out. A small pack

of facial tissues sat nestled in the front right corner of the drawer. To the left, lined up like new fence pickets, were three short stacks of timecards. Each stack was paperclipped and labeled with a sticky note placed squarely in the center of the stack. *Bless Mr. Stevens' neat-freak little heart.*

May, June, and July, the past three months.

Betty heard a stirring behind her and glanced over her shoulder, but saw no one. She was holding her breath. Her pulse pounded in her ears.

Diaz, Fernando's cards were at the top of each stack. Voices from the front rose. Mr. Stevens had entered the building.

Just a quick look at July.

Betty put her finger under the entry for the first day of July. He clocked in at 1001 hours. She slid her finger to the right. He clocked out at 1805. Fernando had worked eight full hours and didn't clock out until six o'clock that evening.

"What are you doing?" Fernando asked from behind Betty.

She yelped and pressed her palm to her chest. "Fernando! You scared me half to death."

He looked at the drawer then back at Betty and narrowed his eyes.

Betty drew out a tissue and waved it in his face. "Looking for a Kleenex." She closed the drawer, slipped past Fernando's frowning gaze, and made a show of blowing her nose on the way back to the main grocery store.

Jacqueline whizzed past her in the canned goods aisle. "Here I am, everybody," she said, her voice as cheerful as a songbird. "Just a little mascara emergency.

All better now."

Betty found one of LB's shoes in the middle of the dairy aisle, but she never found the other. She started for home. One foot scuffed along the pavement in an oversized shoe, and the other foot silently padded along. Her long shadow stumbled before her. She thought about how Julie must be a difficult child to love. And yet, Jacqueline did love her. "A lot," she said to her shadow.

Would I have loved a difficult child if I had become a mother? The envy that clawed at her heart told her that at least she thought she would have. *Lord, forgive me. I should be happy for Jacqueline's motherhood instead of feeling sorry for myself.*

When she got home, Betty threw LB's socks in the dirty clothes and took frozen leftovers out to thaw. Her stomach complained of hunger, but she'd wait for LB to get back so they could eat together.

She sat in her reading chair, missing LB and staring at her phone, willing him to call. Her mind wandered. If Julie really was that bad at home, how'd she get that way? The Ivys were odd, and Jacqueline was shallow, but neither of them had a short temper. Neither of them was prone to violence.

And how did Chad end up such a bad kid? Why couldn't the juvie services help him? Miller always said the TJJD only fostered kids' violence and recklessness. What was our society doing wrong?

She brought up the picture she took of the Polaroid

photo. The dead boy's face grinned–smirked–at the camera.

Did Chad and Julie know each other, both of them being cheerleaders? Chad, especially with his good looks, could have been a bad influence on Julie. But it didn't make sense. She would have had to know him before he was arrested. If he was sixteen at the time of the arrest, she would have only been twelve. How would a twelve-year-old from Tulip even meet a sixteen-year-old from Weatherford?

"Middle school cheerleaders don't cheer at high school games." Her voice echoed without LB's presence to absorb it. She itched to touch his prickly face.

There were no middle school cheerleading camps in Tulip, but...

She scurried to her computer and searched for camps in Weatherford. Bingo. "All Stars Junior Cheer Camp Celebrates Twenty-Five Years." Her shoulders tensed. It was an article in the Weatherford paper about the camp's success and longevity. She held her breath and read, making sure it was just for younger kids.

For members of the East Weatherford High School squad, it's considered a privilege to volunteer as assistant camp counselors.

"Oh, no!" Betty grabbed her phone and punched Jacqueline's number. She took a calming breath as the phone rang. No need to alarm Jacqueline.

"Hel-LO-oh," Jacqueline answered with her typical, sing-song *hello*. "To whom do I have the blessed privilege of speaking?" Bartholomew's euphonious tenor voice was belting "How Great Thou Art" in the background.

"Knock it off, Jacqueline. I'm listed in your contacts. You know it's me." Betty paused, listening to the song. Even through a tinny phone speaker Bartholemew's melody was better than most stuff on the radio. "So, your husband is home." Betty checked her emails while she talked, looking for any message from LB. There was nothing.

"Indeed. Like the Good Book says, *Make music to the Lord with the Bart.*"

Betty cringed. "I think the verse is *harp*, not *Bart*."

"I know, silly. That's just our little family joke."

His voice rose with the refrain, lifting Betty's soul with the notes. If she listened too long, she'd tear up like she did in church whenever he had a solo. "Bartholemew's voice *is* like a harp," she conceded.

"Exactly, see?"

Betty closed her eyes and tried to concentrate. "Did Julie ever go to a cheerleading camp in Weatherford?"

Bartholomew started in on "Victory in Jesus." Sugarpie yapped at something.

"Yes," Jacqueline answered with pride in her voice. "Two years running. Why?"

Betty's jaw went slack. She'd have to tell Miller that Julie and Chad could have known–probably did know–each other. "Um." No need to worry the already stressed woman.

"Why?" Jacqueline asked again, this time with a quiver in her voice.

"I forgot to tell you earlier that your new teal nails are gorgeous." It wasn't a total lie. Teal was one of Betty's favorite colors.

"Thank you *ever* so much, Betty. You should join

me some time at the Nails and Bails."

The salon did bail bonds, too, Betty recalled.

"They have manicurists," Jacqueline said, "who work miracles on even the most hopeless cases."

Betty felt her nostrils flare. "Thanks, Jacqueline. So sorry you have to rush off. Bye now."

"Bye, hon."

Betty sucked in a sharp breath. She knew what had been niggling her earlier. She hadn't actually *seen* Julie in the crowd at the ice cream parlor.

I'm thinking nonsense.

Betty threw her arms up in despair. She sighed, got up, and went out to check the mail.

Another threatening postcard was among the shopping ads and a water bill.

Four words in the same poor penmanship: *Back off or else!*

Once inside, Betty scrutinized the card. It was a generic tourist card with the Abilene skyline and an Abilene postmark. Her thoughts returned to Julie.

Julie could have driven out there in her fancy sports car and picked up a postcard. Did it look like her handwriting?

Betty fetched her folder with the student's poems and laid them out on the kitchen table. There were some students with terrible penmanship like the author of the postcards, but none of the students wrote in cursive. Betty stacked the papers back in her folder, pausing at Sylvia's poem, the baffling one with the odd ending.

Once slept, the darkness drawn, I leapt fools' canyon grand.
Not right, but wrong, the night the theft.

WHEN DID WE LOSE SYLVIA?

*Time swiped the moonroof, and now I see, your
auto-
Cratic love for me.
We went from bliss to being this.*

She smoothed the paper with her palm, and her heart thumped harder. She would have sworn on her parents' graves that she felt Sylvia's young soul weeping from the paper.

Betty was still puzzled as to why Sylvia had chosen to cut *autocratic* in half, leaving *auto-* as a word at the end of a line. The words at the end of each line were the most prominent in any poem.

Betty screeched and slapped her forehead. "Grand theft auto!" she yelled. "Why didn't I see this before?"

She ran to the office and printed off the picture from her phone, then colored Emmie's hair with a black marker. Betty sketched a little tattoo up the girl's cheek.

"Hello, Sylvia."

She quickly dialed Miller's personal number. She didn't bother saying hello. "Emmie Piper and Sylvia Smith are the same person!"

"Betty, there's been a development," he said, apparently ignoring her discovery. His voice was scratchy. He sounded plumb wore out. "Mr. Smith just turned himself in."

Chapter 18

My mood is dark
The sky is gray
My soul despairs
Return, I pray

"Then Sylvia's back!" Betty said over the phone to Miller. She jumped to her feet and danced a little jig. *Thank you, Lord.*

"Uh, Betty." He yawned.

"Is she okay?"

"Betty, listen, please."

"Does she need a place to stay?" The spare room was crammed with LB's model trains, but Betty's little office had a futon, and there was always the couch in the living room if Sylvia preferred that.

Miller didn't answer. Betty heard office chatter and a printer, so she knew he was still on the phone.

"What's wrong?"

"Sylvia didn't come back with Mr. Smith, and he won't tell us where she is."

Betty slumped back in her chair. "But if he confessed, then she'd be innocent, and there'd be no reason for her to stay hidden." Of course, if what Jacqueline said about Mr. Smith being feeble was true, he could have confessed just to cover for Sylvia. And since Betty now knew Emmie and Sylvia were the same person, it's even more plausible that Chad was after Sylvia and that Mr. Smith was covering for his granddaughter. Oh, this was not good, not good at all.

Miller released another yawn. "Floyd's going to keep him here overnight. I'm going home for some shuteye. Maybe Mr. Smith will be more talkative in the morning."

Betty closed her eyes and slowly shook her head. "But she's out there all alone."

He had already hung up.

The first days after her parents had died, Betty was not alone. Not really. There was a social worker who kept patting her hand and offering her water. In quick succession, there were clerical workers filling out paperwork, a guardian ad litem, a pediatrician, her school's principal, her new school's principal, more people filling out paperwork, the pastor's wife, new classmates, new cross country running teammates, and finally, her fosters. So many people had never been so close physically and yet so impalpable. Their lives whisked by, leaving vaporous trails and echoes of conversations that Betty couldn't grab hold of. Her world had gotten bigger and faster, or maybe she had gotten smaller. An unmoored girl, tossed about by the speed wakes of life.

LB wasn't home yet, and supper was thawed, so she put it in the fridge to keep.

She stood at the sidelight, her forehead resting against the glass, and gazed at the grass made black by the night. She imagined Sylvia out there, alone. *I've got to find her.*

She needed to let Miller know about the second postcard, too, but she wasn't about to call and wake him up after he had sounded like a zombie.

A flash of lighting turned the distant stygian sky pale. There was a storm blowing in from the north. That and nightfall dropped the temperature in the house enough that Betty hobbled to the bedroom on still painful feet and dug out a pair of fuzzy socks. She hoped LB was sheltered somewhere, warm and safe asleep and not on the road in the dark with a storm approaching.

Betty returned to the living room and picked up her phone. No, she would *not* text him again in case he was driving. Being too wound up about both Sylvia and LB to sleep, she retreated to her reading chair with her Bible.

She opened it randomly and settled in for a long read. Her thoughts were spinning, her knee bounced, and her wounded feet throbbed. She said a prayer for LB and Sylvia, for Miller and Flora. Julie, Hank, Bridget, Juan. Mr. Smith.

Consider the ravens: for they neither sow nor reap–

She didn't remember reading further.

Betty's phone rang, startling her awake. She pushed the green *accept* button before checking the caller ID.

"LB!" What time was it? The living room window was still dark. "I was worried when you didn't return my text." She limped to the kitchen on one good leg and one leg that was asleep and tingling. At least her feet were feeling better. The microwave said eleven-thirty.

"Uh, no. This is Cletus, Mizz Bell. Mr. Bell's been in an accident. His phone must be somewhere in the wreckage."

"Wreckage?" Betty's throat tightened.

"He's in surgery right now."

A squeak escaped her lips. She punched off, sank to the floor, and called Flora.

Chapter 19

In the mirror it's me I see
I'm wrinkled like a raisin
Stooped as a windblown tree
I'm old as candy cigarettes
I get mail from AARP,
But my mind is sharp
Still witty as can be

"Drive faster, Flora," Betty said. She peered out the windshield into the rainy night. The road looked slick as sweat.

"Really?"

Betty bit down on a rising scream and simply nodded.

The SUV accelerated. Distant lightning turned the sky from black to steel. "If this storm gets too fierce," Flora said, "those lines north of us will get damaged."

When they pulled up to the hospital, Flora stopped against the curb parallel to the visitors' entrance.

"This is as close as I can get to the doors, hon," Flora said, glancing down at Betty's fuzzy socks. "I'll let you out then go park. Got my rain slicker and everything."

Betty dashed through the puddles taking over the entrance patio then ran inside.

A young man at the reception desk asked what she needed, but Betty waived him off. It was a small hospital with only two wings and thirty-six beds. All Betty had to do was sprint down the hall, or both halls if needed, and look for LB as she passed each room.

The corridor was dark to allow patients to sleep. Betty's wet socks splatted the waxed floor tiles as she ran. She hesitated at each doorway.

Is LB in this room? She ran. She slowed. *Is he in that room?*

Her wet feet lost their grip as she reached the end of the first hall, and her hip slammed the hard floor. Her cheek hit the tiles with a pop. She slid like a baseball player stealing second base.

"Mizz Bell!" It was Cletus. He marched out from behind a laundry cart. "Stay put. Are you hurt?"

"I'm fine." She sat up, rubbing her cheek. "Where's LB?"

He pursed his lips. "Well, if you promise not to run through the hallway in wet socks, I'll tell you."

She nodded and stood. When he gave her the room number, Betty strode as fast as she could without breaking into a run. She slowed when she approached LB's room number and heard voices coming from his room.

"Listen, Lug Brain, I just want a straight answer. Did you see any spirits from the other side when you were under anesthesia?" Flora's voice.

"It was dark, I tell you, dark as black velvet at night." LB's voice.

Betty neared the room, joy bursting in her chest at the sound of her husband's voice.

"Then you must have gone to the other place," said Flora.

Anger zapped Betty's joy. She rounded the doorway. "Flora, you take that back!"

LB had one hand in bandages. He flicked his other hand at Flora. "Pay her no mind, Betty. You know how she is."

At the sight of LB's bruised but beautiful face, his legs casually crossed on top of his hospital bed covers, and a Dr. Pepper on his nightstand, Betty's heart sent fuzzy, warm tingles through her chest. "You're okay." Her voice shook with emotion.

He smiled and raised his bandaged hand. "If you think this is bad, you ought to see the pig. Did you know wild pigs' noses are so sensitive that they can smell food buried ten inches underground?"

"Nerd," Flora muttered.

His forehead was speckled with tiny scabs, probably from the shattering of his car's safety glass. He patted the purple flesh around his eye then ran his thumb along his swollen lip, and a serious expression crossed his face. "It feels like the airbag punched me in the face."

He cocked his head to the side and looked at Betty. "Kind of like that shiner you're getting," he said.

Betty's hand went to her cheek. It was starting to throb.

He lifted his bandaged hand. "I've got screws now."

Flora smirked. "You always were a little screwy."

A flash of lightning lit up the room with thunder

quick on its tail.

"You better go home," LB said. "The storm's getting close."

Flora laid her hand on Betty's shoulder. "Lardo Bu–I mean, LB is right. We should go before this sprinkle turns into a downpour."

Betty kissed LB gently on his speckled forehead and left with Flora.

In the morning, Miller called while Betty was reading her soggy newspaper.

"I took Mr. Smith home," he said.

"Did he tell you where Sylvia is? Did you tell him we know Emmie and Sylvia are the same person?"

"Hold your horses, Betty. What's this *we* nonsense? You are a civilian." There was a pause. "But thank you for your theory," he added. "As for Mr. Smith, he didn't make a peep. That's why I'm calling. Why don't you visit him and work that charm of yours and see if you can get him to tell us where Sylvia is holed up."

Betty moved the phone away from her face so she could burp without Miller hearing. She looked down at the stained tee shirt draped over her flat chest and ran her tongue across her not-brushed-yet, fuzzy teeth. "I'm so charming I curdled the milk on my cereal. But sure, I'll go talk to him."

Morning humidity from the storm pressed its way into Betty's pores then evaporated with the rising sun, chilling her skin like a swamp cooler. That was the good thing about cold fronts. They brought thunderstorms, but they brought relief from the heat, too.

The swelling in Betty's feet had gone down, and she was thankful to fit back into her flats again.

The county was supposedly done with repairs on the covered bridge, so Betty took the dirt road. When she approached the structure, she could see some of the wood siding had been replaced, and the whole thing had a fresh coat of barn-red paint.

Sunlight poured from the sky, dotting the dew and turning the grassy landscape into thousands of tiny, golden orbs.

She stopped at the threshold. Maybe it was the time of day, maybe it was the whole idea of a murder in the quiet, little town of Tulip, but Betty could have sworn the inside of the bridge was as dark and foreboding as the shadow of death. Cold air crept out and wrapped around her ankles. She hugged her purse to her chest to chase off the chill.

"I'm being silly." She shouldered her purse and leaned forward as if in a runner's stance before the start of a Marathon. *Though I walk through the valley...* She leapt forward and sprinted into the darkness. Her dress flats clopped the wooden planks like horseshoes. In less than five seconds, she was on the other side, and she laughed in spite of herself until another laugh joined hers in the morning air. "Sylvia?"

Craning her neck in the direction of the laugh, Betty held her breath and listened. But the only sounds she heard were the tick of a grasshopper at her feet and the distant engine noise from Highway 6.

The hairs on her arms rose. She looked back at the bridge and wouldn't have been surprised to see the gray-skinned ghost of the little Sanchez girl. *Darn that Flora, putting spooky thoughts in my head.*

Betty continued on her journey. *This is probably all a waste of time, anyway. Mr. Smith wouldn't let Flora inside when she brought the grapefruit casserole, so why would he let me in?*

Betty was wrong. As soon as Betty introduced herself, the hunched man stepped back, leaning on his cane, and motioned Betty in. She was struck by the youthfulness of his face. He was maybe sixty at the most, trapped in a skeletal prison that was aging far faster than the years were passing.

She followed the stick-thin man into the kitchen. He took baby steps and planted his cane in a careful manner.

The previous two times she'd been in the dilapidated house, she had merely glanced through the entryway of the kitchen. Today, she was pleasantly surprised at the crisp, white countertop tile, the late-model refrigerator, and the bright coat of yellow paint on the smooth walls. A magnet with a toucan's image held a faded photograph. It looked like a woman, but it was hard to tell from where they sat at the little bistro table. If Betty turned to her right, she could see out the front windows of the house. If she turned to the left, she could see blue sky through the kitchen window. The views gave the kitchen a pleasant, airy feel.

The man smelled like arthritis cream and musty bookshelves which prompted Betty to ask, "Where have you and Sylvia been hiding?" Betty asked.

Mr. Smith's rheumy eyes scanned Betty. "Sylvia said you was the only adult who *saw* her," he said, apparently ignoring Betty's question. "You was the reason we moved to Tulip in the first place. She's a big fan of your poetry, Mizz Bell."

The tension fled from Betty's brow. She closed her eyes and smiled, imagining she was hugging the girl.

"Most folks misunderstand Sylvia," Mr. Smith said, interrupting Betty's imaginary hug. "The last place we lived, the man that came to fix the furnace called her a freak." He wiped a gnarled hand across the table as if wiping away the memory. "And the supermarket clerk in Tulip proper is just plain scared of her."

Betty cringed and could imagine Jacqueline's reaction when she first set eyes on her biological child. "Sylvia is a brilliant, artistic girl," she said.

Behind Mr. Smith the new refrigerator gleamed. A score of prescription medicines sat on top. There was an easy-grip jar opener on the tile countertop.

He nodded, a slight move on his hunched neck. "I certainly think she's all that. She wanted to do up the house." Pivoting slightly, he dipped his head toward the countertop. "But this is the only room we got finished before…"

Jacqueline was right. Mr. Smith couldn't have gripped, much less swung, a sledgehammer. *That proves he is covering for someone.*

"Mr. Smith, did Sylvia and Julie get along?" Betty was testing him. She still couldn't recall seeing Julie at the Creamery with the other kids at the time of the murder.

"Who's Julie?"

Betty's chest tightened. He had no reason to take the blame for murder to protect a girl he didn't know. He could be lying about knowing Julie, of course, but he looked more like a beaten man than a conniving liar. There was only one person left, then, that Mr. Smith could be covering for: Sylvia.

Sylvia killed Chad.

Betty swallowed the sob that threatened to erupt from her throat. It was devastating news, but she needed Mr. Smith to tell her where Sylvia was. It'd be better if the girl turned herself in rather than being hunted down by Miller.

The morning chill had made it into the house, and Mr. Smith began shivering. Betty got up and looked in the living room for a jacket or something to drape over his shoulders. She found a black scarf and placed it around his neck.

"Mr. Smith," Betty said, her voice soft. "Tell me about the day Chad Kozlowski died."

"It was self-defense. Yeah, and Sylvia wasn't even here." He looked away and shifted in his seat. "I wouldn't tell the boy where she was, and he got angry."

"But where's Sylvia?"

He shook his head.

"Mr. Smith, I know Chad and Sylvia knew each other."

He looked at her, his eyes wide.

Betty leaned forward. "I think Chad was released

then came here to track down Sylvia."

"Chad, that good for nothing—" He got up and retrieved a much-handled envelope and pulled out the letter inside. "I got this after we lived in Aledo about six months." He read out loud from the letter. "'Old man, you can't hide nobody from us. We'll get you.' And he said some other, unsavory things not fit for a lady's ears." He folded the paper and tucked it into the envelope. "I held onto the letter for the parole board. I didn't want him getting paroled. It worked. He served his full sentence, but when his time was up, he got out, of course."

"I think he threatened your beloved granddaughter. Maybe he grabbed Sylvia or hit her, and you did what you had to to save her life."

Mr. Smith manipulated the scarf with his stiff fingers until it was draped over his head, covering all but a thin slice of his visage. He cried.

"You swung the sledgehammer."

"Yes." He sobbed.

"Except it wasn't you, Mr. Smith, was it? It was Sylvia."

"It was me. I killed the SOB."

Betty glanced at his meds on top of the refrigerator. "I don't believe you."

He grunted and shifted in his seat. "I did, I tell you."

"But Mr. Smith, if it was self-defense, Sylvia won't get in trouble." She gently touched his shoulder. "Please tell me where she is. Think of her out there all alone."

The refrigerator gurgled, and somewhere outside a sparrow fussed.

"You don't understand." He extended his hand toward the aged photograph under the bird magnet. "That's my daughter. She was killed." He said it *kilt* like Miller would, and Betty felt a tug in her heart in the same way she was fond of Miller. "She had so many bullets in her," he continued, "like she was target practice."

Betty's eyes watered. "Sylvia's adoptive mother was shot?" Betty said, putting two and two together.

He grunted. "Adopted? There wasn't no adoption. Where'd you get that idea?"

"I thought… Please, go on."

He used the scarf to wipe his eyes. "Sylvia's mama was shot for no other reason than her boyfriend, Sylvia's dad, tried to quit his own gang and make a real life, be a dad and a husband. They was gonna be married."

Betty laid a hand on his arm. "I'm so sorry. That must be why you sent the postcards warning me off."

He wiped his nose with his sleeve. "Postcards? I don't know nothing about no postcards."

Betty wondered, then, who sent them, but she didn't want to interrupt again.

"Sylvia's daddy, he left to keep Sylvia safe. We ain't never heard from him since." He jabbed his crooked hand at Betty. "And that's why I can't let nobody find her. Those gangs, they's *vengeful* people."

The refrigerator compressor stuttered then restarted, and the microwave beeped. A power fluctuation. The Coop was probably working on downed lines.

"But you don't have to fear Chad's gang. Jane Eyre disbanded soon after he was convicted."

Mr. Smith's mouth fell open. He shook his head.

She leaned forward on her elbows. "It's true. Deputy Miller assured me."

"Really?"

"Yes, honest," Betty said.

Mr. Smith blinked a few times as if trying to take in the news. "I didn't know. I've been so scared." He started laughing, and it turned into deep sobs. "All this time, I didn't know. We've been hiding out at the–"

A sharp *tink* of breaking glass followed immediately by a crack so loud Betty could feel it in her chest interrupted Sylvia's grandfather.

Betty spun toward the noise. "That's crazy." She let out a nervous laugh and rushed to the front of the house. "It sounded like a rifle. Who'd hunt so close to a house?" She pulled up short when she saw a hole in the window. Was somebody shooting at them?

She ran back to the kitchen. "We've gotta get down. I'll call 911." She fished her phone out of her pocket. Grabbing his arm, she tried to pull him to the floor, but his dead weight fell face-first onto the table. She brushed aside the black scarf. A neat, round hole pierced the side of his head.

"Mr. Smith!" Betty screamed. She staggered and fell to her knees. *Suck it up, Glenniford,* her college running coach used to say. Betty mentally leaned on her coach's words, said a quick prayer for strength, then gritted her teeth and pressed her fingertips on Mr. Smith's carotid artery. She waited.

A grasshopper landed on the kitchen window with a *tick*.

There was no pulse. *Rest in peace, Mr. Smith.*

A fire of rage grew in Betty's chest. He had been

ready to tell Betty where Sylvia was, and someone *killed* him, and now *nobody* knows where she is! Betty jumped to her feet with a growl. She burst out the front door and sprinted in the direction the bullet had come from.

Her dress flats slid on the loose rocks of the driveway and roadway. When she realized she was out in the open with a murderer nearby, Betty ducked behind a scrub oak and listened. Footsteps crashed through the brush. She followed. *Not too close, just close enough to get a glimpse.*

From ahead, an *oof!* came. The footsteps momentarily stopped.

It sounded like a female had fallen. Betty remembered the laugh at the covered bridge and how at first she hoped it was Sylvia. Betty shook her head in denial. *But it can't be Sylvia. She wouldn't kill her own grandfather!*

"Sylvia?" Betty called out, ignoring her reservations. "Wait up!'

There was no answer, just footsteps resuming, this time toward Betty's right.

Betty chased the sound. The ground had vegetation here. It was easier for her shoes to get a grip, but she wasn't getting closer to the fleeing footsteps. She turned up the speed, pumping her arms and driving her knees. It sounded like the shooter was running to Betty's left now, and she turned that direction, racing past mesquite, bunch grass, boulders, cacti.

After a good minute at sprint speed, Betty hadn't gotten closer, and her own breathing was getting so loud she couldn't hear the shooter's footsteps anymore. She gave up.

She came to a stop and rested with her hands on her knees, catching her breath.

She needed to call Miller, but when she reached in her pocket for her phone, it wasn't there. It was back at the Sanchez house, keeping vigil over Mr. Smith's body. Along with her purse and house keys.

She didn't want to go back there, but she had no choice. Looking around, she tried to get her bearings. There were a lot of sizable rocks and low brush she had run through. "Lucky I didn't step on a rattlesnake." She'd have to pick her way carefully back to the road.

"Which is that way." She pointed and hoped.

Betty emerged from the scrub brush at the creek. The covered bridge was in sight. She had her bearings now. Betty scurried up the creek bank to the road and turned toward the Sanchez house.

She didn't want to look again at Mr. Smith slumped over the table... with a *hole* in his head. Her gaze fixed on the floor, Betty dragged herself into the kitchen and snatched her purse and phone from the little table. She dashed outside and dialed Miller's direct number. "Someone killed Sylvia's grandfather. I'm at the Sanchez place right now."

"Don't touch anything. We're on our way."

Betty waited in the driveway for Miller. He arrived in a flurry of flashing lights with Deputy Floyd arriving a moment later.

"I think it was a woman," Betty said. "The voice sounded female when she fell. And there was a girl's laugh at the bridge earlier."

"Same voice?"

"Actually, now that I think about it, no. The voice at the bridge was younger, childlike."

Flora would have insisted it was the Sanchez girl's ghost.

Miller's gaze scanned the roadway and the brush beyond. "I reckon at the creek that was kids playing. But the older voice..." He frowned at her. "You shouldn't be chasing after killers with guns."

Betty looked at her feet. "I just wanted to get a glimpse, but I couldn't catch up."

Miller took a step back. "You mean whoever it was outran *you?*"

With a huff, Betty said, "Obviously, it was someone younger. I am a middle-aged woman, Deputy, no spring chicken."

Stepping out of the house, Deputy Floyd said, "Coroner's on her way."

After nodding at Deputy Floyd, Miller said, "Well, did you recognize the shooter's voice?"

"It was familiar, but I've lived in Tulip for thirty-some years. A couple hundred voices sound familiar." Betty gauged the distance between the nearest brush and the front of the house. "It'd have to be a woman who's really good with a rifle to shoot from out there," she said, pointing at the brush across the road.

"Eh." Miller shrugged. "That'd be half of Tulip, age twelve and up. Folks taking out coyotes who threaten calves or shooting wild pigs who dig trenches in their yards." Tapping his notepad, he said, "Ya know, it could have been Sylvia."

Betty glared at him. "No, I don't believe that! Why would she kill her own grandfather?"

"Because she thought instead of turning himself in, he was turning her in."

Betty refused to believe that. Even if Sylvia did think her grandfather was turning her in, she wouldn't kill her last family on earth. She'd be all alone. And that was scary, Betty knew. No one would do that on purpose.

She turned away from him. "May I go now, *Deputy?*"

"Sure, but we're gonna need your shoes."

Betty let out a grunt. If she were a cussing woman, this would be the time.

"Floyd, bring an evidence bag then take Mizz Bell home."

"Take me by the Goodwill first," she said, casting a slight sneer at Miller. "I need to buy a pair of shoes."

Once home, and wearing her new-old, lime-green, sequined sneakers (there wasn't much of a selection in her duck-footed size at the Goodwill), Betty was more determined than ever to find Sylvia before Miller and the law did and things got worse, scarier, and traumatic for the girl.

But where to look?

She called the hospital to check on LB then got her lesson plan together for tomorrow. All the while her brain was trying to figure out where Sylvia could be hiding.

Near the end of class the next day, Betty wrote a note to the summer receptionist, who wouldn't even be back in the building until Monday, falsely claiming she had lost her sunglasses and would Pearly (the receptionist) be a dear and let her know if the sunglasses showed up.

"I need a volunteer from the class." Julie's hand shot up higher and faster than the others, just as Betty suspected it would. "Thank you, Julie. Please take this to the admin office and drop it in Pearl Landry's mailbox."

As soon as the girl bounced out the door, Betty counted to ten then dismissed the class. "Hank, a moment, please." She motioned him toward her desk.

"Have you heard from Sylvia?"

"No, she doesn't like social media. Says people stalk you on social media."

And not having a social media presence makes it harder for gang members to track you down. "Tell me more about her."

Hank sucked in his lips and looked away.

"Was she scared of anyone?"

He looked at her.

"Are you still worried Julie will find out about your date? After all, you said it was *not* a date, and now that Julie knows about your horticultural interests..."

He rolled his eyes at the mention of the greenhouse

episode. "Well, I dunno if it'll help," he said, "but like I said before, she likes birds. And the color black. Oh, and she likes to draw Slinkys."

"Slinkys?"

Julie burst into the room. "There you are, Hunk. Everybody's leaving. Let's go.

"Said she was learning her O's," he said to Betty.

Betty's heart stuttered then slammed into high gear. That's it! She was the only student who didn't complain about Betty's cursive. Sylvia must be learning cursive herself. The horrible penmanship, but not with a shaky hand...

Betty bid Julie and Hank goodbye and gathered her papers.

Sylvia wrote the postcards.

Betty hurried home, thankful that the post-storm temperatures were still relatively mild, and she *could* hurry.

When she got inside, she brought up images of the first postcard on her phone and compared them to the recent postcard. She had forgotten to tell Miller about the second one, but to her credit, she had meant to tell him the night she called, the night Mr. Smith turned himself in.

One from a cheap motel in Fort Worth, to the east of Tulip. One from Abilene with the Abilene skyline and Hotel Wooten in the distance, to the west of Tulip. If Mr. Smith–God rest his soul–had been trying to hide after Chad's murder, then it'd make sense to move around. "And change cars," she added, remembering Mr. Smith's abandoned car on the interstate. "Sylvia, you are in Abilene."

She texted Flora. *Can you take me to Abilene?*

When Flora didn't answer right away, Betty requested an Uber ride, but there were no drivers available. In other words, Cletus was at the hospital.

The phone rang. It was Miller.

"Floyd said you left green sequins in his car."

Flora finally texted back. *On a date. He drove me to the Hilton museum in Cisco.* She added a heart emoji.

Flora's on a date?

"I'm trying to talk to a frightened orphan child," Betty said to Miller, "and you all are worried about sequins in your cruisers?"

There was a pause. "What do you mean *talk* to her? Sylvia Smith is a person of interest in two murders. If you know where she is–"

"I didn't mean to say *talk*. I meant... She's a child, Miller, alone and scared." Betty still had Flora's car keys. It'd be so easy to walk over to Flora's house and borrow her Blazer. *But I don't drive.*

"You know where she is?"

Visions of tire skidding, of metal folding and people getting crushed, flooded Betty's brain. "She's in..." She tried to speak despite the terrible images swirling in her head. *Abilene*, Betty mouthed.

"Now, quit being a doggone rusty screw and tell me where she's hiding!" There was a pause. "Betty," he said, his voice all business-like now, "where is Sylvia Smith?"

Focusing her gaze on the keys, she stood straighter, then hung up without answering the deputy's question. She grabbed her purse and marched out the door. She was headed for Abilene.

Chapter 20

The woman chose a little nook
Spectacles on, she opened the book.
It was louder on the inside
Shouts of battle, the kingdom defend!
She closed the book, 'twas silent again.

Betty put her phone on silent so it couldn't distract her. She slipped it in her purse then tossed her purse over the center console of Flora's Blazer and onto the passenger-side floor. Then she crammed her long frame behind the steering wheel. The seat was pushed forward to fit Flora's short legs. Any further forward and Betty would be sitting on the hood. She located the seat adjustment and slid it back.

She adjusted the mirrors like her driving instructor had taught her to do all those years ago. "Like riding a bicycle," she said, her voice quaking. Within five minutes, she was on the 75 miles-per-hour interstate going 40.

Her lungs were concrete. It was impossible to get a full breath. Bright, afternoon sunlight fell on the road, and the asphalt mutated into watery waves in the distance. An eighteen-wheeler passed, its rumble vibrating Betty's chest. Her hands clenched the steering wheel, and she accelerated to 50.

Having gone to school at Abilene Christian, Betty knew how to get to the zoo, and thus the aviary where Sylvia probably was. "Among her bird friends."

But an aviary was too easy, Betty decided somewhere near Cisco. (By that time, she was zipping along at 52 miles-per-hour and had learned how to breathe again.) Sylvia–*Emmie*–was smarter than that. She wouldn't hide in an obvious place.

Betty had a better place to look.

In quick succession, three cars passed as if she were standing still. Betty cringed when she imagined the consequences of a wreck at their speed. She had the sense that someone was following her, but she couldn't tell. It'd mean taking her eyes off the road to look in the rearview mirror, and as long as the car was still moving, she wasn't about to do that. Besides, she had squared things with Jacqueline after Miller had taken her in for questioning, so there was no one left to follow her.

Well, she rationalized, a whole lot of people were *following* her. Two cars zipped past. *And then they go around me.*

She spotted the sign for the zoo, but she headed toward the Robert E. Howard Memorial Library instead. When she pulled into a parking place, the car straddled two spots, but she wasn't about to try again. It took a minute to pry her fingers off the wheel and shift into park. She cut the engine, leaving the keys dangling. "Yes!" she screamed at the headliner. "Yes, yes, yes!"

She leaped from the Blazer and swung the door shut. She gawked at Flora's car. "I *drove*," she said, throwing her shoulders back then giving the Blazer's window a high-five.

A second later, another car door slammed in the next row over. She had to wait for two compact cars to drive past before she could make her way across the parking lot. *Busy place.*

Once inside, Betty paused for a moment while her eyes adjusted to the dimmer interior light. To the right of the checkout stand, the children's section called to the youngest patrons with its short, primary-colored bookshelves. The shelves surrounded a play area with blocks and wooden trains. Animal mobiles turned slowly under the air conditioner vents. A woman pulled a lemon-yellow and cherry-red board book from a shelf and added it to the stack in her arms. At a small table sat a boy about eleven years old. His head rested on his folded arms. He was very much asleep. A little girl stood at an even smaller table with a Sandra Boynton book balanced on her head. The book fell.

Sylvia was not in the children's section.

Betty went to the left of the checkout stand.

She passed a row of computers. A middle-aged man was looking at a web page titled *Job Openings.*

In the young adult section, two bendy teens crouched low to the floor, their heads leaning at an angle that would allow faster reading of spines. They yoga-d their way along the titles.

Betty headed for the sign that indicated the adult fiction area.

Once there, she spotted a young couple in matching upholstered chairs by a window, he with a magazine and she with a hardcover. Their feet were entwined. A woman in reading glasses huddled in a nook with a paperback. A preschool-aged boy zipped between the tall shelves in front of Betty. He was clutching a wooden train engine.

Betty looked left and right then behind her, expecting the child's parent to follow in pursuit. The bill of a baseball cap disappeared around the edge of a shelf. It was probably the child's older brother or short father tracking down the exuberant boy.

She ignored the D's and C's but stopped at the B's. Sylvia wasn't there. Betty's chest deflated. How silly of her to assume Sylvia would be reading Bronte at the library. *As if I had actually gotten to know the girl after a handful of classes, a similar number of poems, and short chats with those who did know her.*

She pressed her lips together. *But you can get to know people through their poetry!* Besides, Mr. Smith–an involuntary shiver ran up her spine when she thought of the man and the hole in his head–even smelled like a library.

Still, she had been wrong. Sylvia was not here.

Holding her arm out to the side, she slid her index finger along the B-author spines and walked the length of the shelf. She stopped at *Villette* and pulled it from the shelf. After reading a few lines, she had an urge to read more, especially since she didn't like the thought of getting back in the car to return to Tulip. She'd find an empty reading nook and... Of course! Sylvia wouldn't read in the middle of the aisle.

Betty put the book back then hurried to the alcoves where she had seen the woman with glasses reading. There were a good dozen reading nooks to check. The first two were empty. The third, the same woman was still reading her paperback. The fourth, a study carrel with a college-aged man and several thick books.

A movement of black caught her eye. It was Sylvia racing for the door.

"Sylvia, wait!" Betty ran after her. Footsteps fell in behind Betty. She had probably drawn the attention of a security guard.

Betty slammed through the heavy doors, ran down three steps, then jumped two more. She was glad her new sequined shoes had good, grippy soles.

Sylvia disappeared around the corner of the building.

Turning up the speed, Betty followed. She was sure she could catch someone wearing baggy cargo pants and clodhoppers.

When Betty rounded the corner, Sylvia was at the side street about to cross motionless traffic at a stoplight.

"Wait, Sylvia," Betty yelled. "You're not in trouble." It was hard to yell and run at the same time.

Sylvia wove in and out of idling cars. When Betty ran into the road, the light turned green. Stutter-stepped and dodged while Sylvia widened the gap. A driver in a red pickup truck honked at her. She made it across and heard the same horn honk again.

When she glanced over her shoulder, she saw someone in jeans and a hat following. The dad of the little boy in the library? Why would the boy's dad be following her? Betty decided it was merely a coincidence that someone crossed the street right after she did.

"You're not in trouble, Sylvia," Betty yelled again between her increasingly harder breaths. She was rapidly gaining. They sped past a fountain, a bus stop, a dumpster, a street vendor, and a man sitting on a bench.

His head pivoted as Betty ran by. "Pretty shoes, lady!"

"Wait, Sylvia, please." Betty's legs were burning. They were approaching the Amigone Mortuary. (Betty never did like that name.) "Emmie!"

Sylvia stumbled. She glanced back with big, surprised-looking eyes. Then she took off again. Her thick shoes were landing hard. She was obviously fatigued. She took a sharp left.

Betty tried to follow, but when she turned, Sylvia was gone.

Amigone was directly ahead. It was a historic, cube-shaped, three-story building of limestone with ancient boxwoods along the foundation and corbels along the roof. Betty jogged up the walkway to the front entrance, looking left and right for the girl. Not paying attention to where she was stepping, Betty tripped on the front steps. She heard a pop and felt her ankle turn unnaturally. She tried to get up but could not put weight on her foot.

"Psst, Mrs. Bell, down here." Betty peered to the side of the stairs. There was a three-foot gap between the back of the boxwoods and the building. Sylvia was crouched in the space. Sweaty ropes of hair hung about her face. The untended roots were blonde.

Betty half-crawled beneath the railing and half fell off the edge of the steps. She landed on her back. Holding her injured foot, she gasped with pain.

Sylvia grabbed Betty under the armpits and pulled her further back against the building. The rocky soil smelled like animal droppings and leaf mold.

Sylvia's gaze darted about. Her face was sweating.

She picked up a softball-sized stone and raised it as if to strike.

Chapter 21

We walked, my love
And talked and stroked each other's souls
I laughed and gazed into your eyes
But you were looking somewhere else

"Sylvia, no!" Betty raised her hands in self-defense.

Sylvia shushed her. Her gaze went to the bit of stairs still visible. Then she scooted forward and peered through the shrub.

"Sylvia, honey, it's just me. Put the rock down." Betty's ankle was burning. She tried to smile. "You're safe now."

"No," she said. "I'm not safe. I'm never safe."

Betty reached out and gently wrapped her fingers around Sylvia's arm, then lowered it, but Sylvia didn't let go of the rock.

"I know you testified against Chad Kozlowski in Weatherford. I know he came after you when he was released. He wanted revenge."

"No," she said, shaking her head vigorously. "No, no."

"I know it was self-defense, *Emmie*."

Sylvia dropped the rock. "Yes, I killed him. I mean no, I didn't kill him. Grandpa did."

"Honey, I've met your grandfather. He couldn't lift a sledgehammer much less swing it. Deputy Miller knows that, too."

Sylvia blinked rapidly. She pulled her knees to her chest.

"Listen," Betty said in a soft voice. "You don't have to hide anymore. The Jane Eyres disbanded."

At the mention of the gang's name, Sylvia tensed. "No, that's impossible."

"You're safe now."

"I can never be safe." Tears welled in Sylvia's eyes.

"Your ex-boyfriend is dead, and his gang doesn't exist anymore. Deputy Miller said so. You can live in the open." Betty scanned the girl's raven locks and black, winter-like clothes. "You don't have to walk around disguised as someone else."

Tension eased from the girl's face. "How do you know Chad was my boyfriend?"

"I didn't at first. It was something Bridget said about your grand theft auto poem."

"Grand theft–you figured it out?"

Betty nodded.

"I like Bridget."

"So do I," Betty said. She held out her hand. "Let's go back to Tulip. We'll talk to Deputy Miller together." *And talk about your grandfather and where you're going to stay.*

Sylvia closed her eyes as if considering it. Betty reached for her pocket to grab her phone and call

Miller. It wasn't there. She didn't have her purse, either. Her stomach dropped. In her inexperience, she had left her phone and purse in the unlocked car. And the keys in the ignition.

Someone crashed through the boxwood. "There you are!" Julie yelled. She was wearing a baseball cap with her hair tucked inside. Dots of blood began to grow where the boxwood branches had scratched her face. Her mouth drew up in a sneer, and she lunged for the stone Betty had persuaded Sylvia to drop. Betty scrambled for it, too, but her ankle gave out, and Julie got there first.

"He shouldn't like you," Julie said to Sylvia. Spittle flew from her lips as she talked. It was the same timbre of the shooter's voice, the shooter who had fallen in the scrub brush near the Smiths' house.

Sylvia whimpered and tucked herself into the fetal position.

Anger bloomed in Betty. She swung the heel of her hand at the rock, trying to knock it out of Julie's hand. Julie was too quick and kneed Betty in the nose. Betty rolled backwards to her bottom.

"Nuh-uh-uh," Julie said with a mocking tone.

Betty's nose felt like it was buzzing. And swelling fast. Her bruised cheek from yesterday started throbbing all over again. "But why did you..." Betty caught herself. Sylvia didn't know her grandfather was dead.

"Why'd I kill the old man?" Her voice sounded cold, like sleet on a tin roof. "I saw him through the window. You were sitting at the table with him, and he had a black thing hanging over his head. I thought it was *you*," she said, turning her gaze to Sylvia.

Betty scooted over, trying to somehow get between Julie and Sylvia. It wasn't working. A grasshopper crawled on its backwards-jointed legs beneath one of the boxwoods. Betty remembered the day she nervously stood in front of the class for the first time. *How'd things go from there to here?*

"Why don't you put the rock down, Julie? We're all adults. We can talk about it." Betty grasped for things to say. "Words matter, Julie. *Your* words matter."

Sylvia uncurled her body. "You mean Grandpa is dead?" She sat up. Her arms fell limp at her sides, apparently forgetting her safety. She let out a heartrending wail, and that's when Julie swung the stone.

It all happened in slow motion. Betty could see the trajectory of the rock, how it'd end up slamming into the side of Sylvia's head. Betty's good leg kicked out before the word *kick* could even form in her mind, a protective instinct, a *motherly* instinct. Her lime-green, sequined sneakers landed squarely on Julie's solar plexus. The girl dropped the rock and doubled over, gulping for air that would be a few moments coming.

Betty shoved the stone out of Julie's reach and wrapped her arms around the weeping Sylvia. "I know, honey, I know." *I know what it's like to be all alone in the world.* Betty moved her hands to Sylvia's shoulders and pushed her away. "But you've got to go now. Get to safety. Call the police." Julie's face was purple. A wheeze escaped her lips.

When Sylvia made no move to leave, Betty yelled, "Run!"

"I can't leave you with her." Sylvia's words were blubbery.

Betty rose, balancing on one leg. Sylvia stood too. "I'll be fine," Betty said, "but I can't keep up with you. Go!"

Julie would be on her feet, too, in a hot second. And she'd be mad as Hades. Could Betty incapacitate the girl again? Unlikely.

Betty was becoming woozy with pain. She would try to escape though she knew she wouldn't get very far hopping on one foot. Betty gave Sylvia a push. "Go."

Sylvia finally nodded. She moved toward the stairs.

Julie's hand shot out, grabbed Sylvia's foot, and yanked her off balance. Sylvia screamed as she fell.

"They're back here!" a man yelled.

Miller?

Miller and two Abilene police officers pushed through the boxwood. They were out of breath.

It's getting crowded back here.

Julie swung that blasted rock again, but Miller caught her arm. "Oh no you don't, Miss Ivy."

One of the police officers cuffed Julie while the other skimmed his gaze over Betty. His mouth was agape. "You mean to tell me an old lady outran us?" He inclined his head toward Betty. "Uh, no offense, ma'am."

"Told you she was fast," Miller said.

"No offense taken, officer," Betty said. She was hugging Sylvia and rubbing her back. "I'm just glad both girls are safe now."

Chapter 22

Forgotten rooms where shadows
Skim the floors in shapes
Of icy air, a graceful ghost

Betty polished the last fender. Her arms ached, pain stabbed her back, and she was sure her ears were sunburned. It was Friday, almost two weeks since she borrowed Flora's SUV and went after Sylvia. Amazingly, Flora's car was exactly where Betty had left it, keys in the ignition and purse resting on the floor.

Betty hoped this chore of penance would pass Flora's inspection.

Flora was lounging on her secondhand Adirondack chair under the ash tree in her front yard and studying something on her phone. Betty limped over to join her in the shade. Betty's sprained ankle no longer hurt, but it was still stiff.

When Flora didn't look up, Betty cleared her throat, a pitiful sound. She was thirsty as heck. "Is my wash and wax job suitable?" Betty asked. She had removed years of dust and insects and had waxed and buffed the finish until the car's blue paint looked as deep as an ocean and as shiny as Jacqueline's fake nails.

Flora took her gaze off the phone. She sucked in a big breath. "Why Betty, I didn't know my car could ever look that good again!"

"Then do you forgive me for stealing your car?"

"Oh, I was never mad at you. I just used it as an excuse to get a free car wash. You may borrow it anytime you like."

Shaking her head, Betty said, "I'm prohibited from applying for a driver's license for twenty-four months. I consider that and a hefty fine a pretty lenient deal from the county attorney."

Turning her phone screen toward Betty, Flora said, "You know how ghostly orbs streak across the camera in ghost-hunting shows?"

"No."

"Well, I set up my own ghost camera in the back yard–because you know the Bakers had their people buried back there before I bought the place, and they had the bodies moved because my grandpappy and Bobby Baker's aunt Violet had a falling out over her coonhounds–"

"Well, they were Blueticks after all," Betty said, and then chastised herself for encouraging Flora.

"Exactly, no wonder Violet Baker pitched a fit. Anyway, do you know what my camera caught?"

Betty leaned forward to see Flora's phone screen.

"At eleven o'clock last night, it caught an orb that morphed into a couple of ghost streakers alright. They ran through my back yard naked and waving Texas Tech jerseys."

They watched the video.

"Flora!" Betty wanted to slap her silly. "Those aren't ghosts. First of all, your so-called orb is a moth near the camera lens." She tapped Flora's phone to stop the video. Pointing at the two figures on the screen, Betty said. "And *those* two streakers are Elrod and Lily Grace. You know Elrod is a diehard Red Raiders fan."

"Oh." Flora's shoulders drooped. "I guess there was the season kickoff game last night."

Betty took in what she was seeing on Flora's phone. "Good heavens, they're buck naked." Betty squinted at the black-and-white image of Lily Grace, her head thrown back, her mouth open and smiling as if in mid-laugh. One hand held a jersey above her head. The other was caught in Elrod's grasp. The couple looked ecstatic.

Flora closed the app. "Maybe my camera will catch something tonight," she said. "Hey, are you all done teaching?"

"I have one class left, tomorrow."

"Did you know," LB said, coming up behind Betty as she waited for their breakfast toast to pop up, "there are seven million adopted Americans?"

It was the last Saturday of August, the last day of class. She leaned back against her husband of thirty-five years, letting her arms go limp. They still ached from the car detailing she had done the day before. His face stubble tickled her neck.

"And Sylvia will make seven million and one," she

said. Betty twisted to face him. "LB, are you sure you want to go through with the adult adoption?"

"Think of it more as a business deal," he said.

She playfully slapped his shoulder. "Oh hush." Two pieces of toast popped up, and she took to them with a knife and butter.

"I'm serious." He grabbed the first buttered toast. "Sylvia will have a place to stay while she attends Cisco Community College, and we will have someone who can eventually choose our nursing home."

She took a bite of her own toast. "Grab the milk and cereal, Leopard Butt." Pinching his bottom through his pajama pants, she pictured his adorable birthmark-spattered gluteus maximus then headed for the kitchen table.

They sat down, and he pointed his half-eaten toast at her nose. "You're good with her. You're going to make a great mother."

Betty's breath caught. *A mother.* After all these years, after all that prayer (that begging), she was finally going to be a mother. Funny thing is, if she had become a mother when she and LB were first married, she would have smothered the poor child with overindulgences and over-involved parenting to make up for what she had missed. Betty could see that now.

Warmth danced through her chest, and she squeezed LB's arm. "God's timing is perfect."

They split the paper and ate and read in silence. A local headline caught Betty's eye.

COMPLAINTS FROM TULIP RESIDENTS PROMPT MAYOR TO REMOVE CHICKEN FEATHERS

Tulip's Mayor Buford Helper acquiesced to citizens' demands to remove chicken feathers from his Cadillac. Among those in opposition to the mayor's tribute to his late bodyguard is Jacqueline Ivy. "It's so gauche," Ivy states. "Buford says he did it to honor Roberta, but what idiot thinks chicken feathers on a car would honor a dead bird? The mayor should have thought this through and glued them on his airplane instead," she says, referring to the mayor's single-engine Cessna 172. "At least planes fly."

Reluctantly agreeing to the citizens' demands, Mayor Helper hired Elrod Snew Cooter to remove the feathers. Cooter soaked the feathers in acetone to loosen the cyanoacrylate-based glue. An unfortunate side effect was removal of the car's forest green paint.

Cooter and Helper are second cousins, but so far there have been no complaints from Tulip citizens regarding nepotism for the hiring of Cooter. Elrod Snew Cooter is also the brother to Homer Cooter of the A1 Synergy Energy Electric Cooperative. Homer is quick to add that he was an adoptee after having been left on his parents' front porch by firemen. "So I'm not blood kin to either Buford or Elrod.

Betty accepted LB's offer to drive her to the final class. Her abused arms wouldn't have to carry her book bag, and her stiff ankle meant her gait was slow. "Let's swing by the grocery store first," she said.

When Betty and LB entered the grocery store, Jacqueline was at her stand, singing a round of "Jesus Loves Me" with Mama Teach. The older woman's arms were thrown wide while Jacqueline bounced on her toes. Katydids had better musical talent than either of the two, but their joyful noise made Betty press her hand against her heart and smile, nonetheless.

Miller, out of uniform, was waiting in line with his buggy. LB stayed by the entrance while Betty came around and said hello to Miller.

"You never told me how you and Flora found the photograph of Chad Kozlowski and Emmie Piper," Miller said, his voice low. Betty had to lean in to hear him above the singing.

Betty recalled running upstairs in the Smith house, chasing after a noise that sounded like a girl's laugh. "A ghost told us." She broke out laughing, but when she looked at Miller, his lips were pressed in a hard line, and he was nodding as if taking the news seriously.

"You'll get your shoes back next week," he said, glancing at her feet. His face took on a slight grimace. "There's something else, Betty. I had to send samples from Ben's case to Austin for additional testing."

"But he died from exposure during the ice storm. Everyone knows that."

Miller shook his head. "Sara Higgins insists her son hated the cold. Says he never would have left the house on a night like that." His gaze drifted, and he narrowed his eyes. "Something fishy going on there."

The song ended, and Jacqueline said, "Betty, come here. Let me hug you."

Betty excused herself from Miller's presence with a quick nod then submitted to Jacqueline's clutches. She wondered if she would have been as gracious a mother if someone had kicked her daughter in the stomach.

Toting a bonus-sized box of diapers under his arm, Mr. Smelly joined Jacqueline's checkout line. His skin was more ruddy than usual, and purple shadows under his eyes spoke volumes. Betty said a quick prayer that the baby would sleep through the night tonight.

"Betty," Jacqueline said, her voice gushing with excitement, "you wouldn't believe Julie's new room at the psychiatric rehab center. They let Bart paint it her favorite color, tropical lime. Only the best for our Julie."

I bet a donation from Bart made that happen. Betty cast a glance at LB, and he rolled his eyes.

"Kind of like the color of your sneakers," Jacqueline continued as she looked down at Betty's feet. "I used to have a pair just like them." Looking up again, she raised her chin and fluffed her hair. "Of course, green sequins are *so* last year. *This* year's Carmine Caskcut's Kicks color is tumbling tangerine."

Betty's shoulders and neck stiffened. She stared at Jacqueline. She had intended to let Jacqueline know that she couldn't possibly be Sylvia's birth mother. That Sylvia was raised by her true birth mother until the woman was killed. That Sylvia's natural hair color was blonde. That Jacqueline could quit looking over her shoulder, quit worrying about being blackmailed.

"Hey LB," she said instead, "I'm ready to go now." She gave Mama Teach a quick hug, waved goodbye to Miller and Juan's father, and walked out in her *so* last year's lime-green, sequined sneakers.

It was almost time for class to start. Bridget and Juan interlaced their fingers below their pushed-together desks. She had started to show. Odessa Lynn and Jorge chatted. The twins played tic-tac-toe. Sylvia wasn't there yet.

Sylvia had been staying with Betty and LB and nursing her grief over her grandfather. LB had joined her in building birdhouses, and they were retiling the bathroom together. Sylvia had left the house early that morning for a meeting with Deputy Floyd to review and sign yet more paperwork regarding Chad's death.

Meanwhile, the kids kept eying Julie's empty seat.

"Don't worry, class," Betty said. "Julie's in the best available medical facility."

"In Dallas," Darlene said.

"In a loony bin," Odessa Lynn clarified.

"Now now, Odessa Lynn." Betty gave the girl a stern look. "Julie is receiving the type of care she needs."

The twins nodded, and Bridget said, "Amen to that."

"That's cool how you saved Goth girl's life, Mrs.

B," Juan said. He let go of Bridget's fingers and leaned back in his chair with his hands behind his head. "You know, I've been thinking. Even though you sometimes preach, and your assignments make us reach, you're almost as good as Mama Teach."

The cheerleader row clapped, Hank whistled, and even old-man Jorge let out a whoop.

Betty swallowed a lump in her throat.

Sylvia and Deputy Floyd walked in during the applause. "Why, thank you!" Sylvia said, laughing.

The students turned and gawked at Sylvia as Floyd waved at Betty and slipped out.

Sylvia took the same seat she had before, her tattooed cheek turning slightly pink with everyone's eyes upon her. Trading in her black turtleneck for a black, scoop-neck tank top made her look less Goth.

Actually, no it didn't, decided Betty. It was hard to get past the face tattoo and the combat boots.

The girl had even taken a bottle of Clorox to her hair, stripping it of its stygian color, but the result was an unfortunate shade of urine with flaxen roots. With her pale shoulders, she looked more ghoulish than ever.

And Betty loved her from her pale roots to her sturdy, rubber soles.

When the two of them, along with LB, were at the county courthouse for a pre-adoption session with the judge, Sylvia explained her legal name was "Sylvia Smith" ever since her grandfather had become her guardian. He'd told her she'd be safer that way. Her grandfather had chosen *Smith*, probably because it'd be easier to get lost in the crowd with that name, and she'd chosen *Sylvia* after Sylvia Plath.

"And when did you get interested in birds?" LB

asked.

"After reading Daphne Du Maurier's 'The Birds.' Birds are really smart, you know."

"I don't doubt it," Betty said, remembering what she had learned about chickens when helping out Lily Grace. Betty tilted her head and looked at the girl. "Why do you like the classics so much?"

Sylvia shrugged. "I guess I'm an old soul."

Betty pursed her lips in thought. She still wasn't sure she believed in ghosts, but she was definitely not ready to believe in reincarnated souls.

Returning her attention to the class, Betty asked for students to read their poems. She was surprised Sylvia had one ready. Betty perched at the edge of her chair when Sylvia began to read. Would it be about classic authors, the approach of autumn, or the obvious subject, Sylvia's feathered friends?

It was about ghosts.

Betty sank back in her chair and tried to keep a pleasant expression.

After class, Darlene gave her some homemade deer jerky. Mrs. Smelly pulled her car up to the curb. Juan and Bridget climbed in back on either side of the baby's car seat. Hank approached Betty's desk with his hands in his pockets. He sucked in both of his lips and looked out the window.

"My dad is talking to me again," he said after a moment.

"Good, Hank, good."

He turned and looked at her. "You made it, you know, kinda okay to go after my own dreams. After dinner last night Dad gave me his mother's gardening journal. She died before I was born. I didn't even know she was a gardener."

"That must be exciting to learn, Hank."

"Yes ma'am. Well, me and Darlene are going to Midtown Creamery."

"It's not a date!" she yelled from the doorway as they left.

The rest of the cheerleaders left on bicycles or strolled together in pairs. The twins thanked Betty in perfect English before heading out to Jorge's car. Jorge himself shook her hand and said he was going to study for the GED.

Betty smiled. "It'll be difficult, but I think you can do it."

When only Betty and Sylvia remained, the girl rose and stretched. "Ready to go, Mom?"

Mom! Joy circled her heart and made it dance. She felt weightless. Her stomach was floating.

Sylvia scrunched her nose. "No, *Mom* doesn't sound right."

Betty's stomach came crashing down. "I'm sure it feels–"

"That's what I called my birth mom before she died."

Betty forced her lips into a smile, trying to hide her disappointment. "I understand, Sylvia."

They left the building together.

At the end of the sidewalk, Sylvia slipped her arm around Betty's waist and leaned her head on Betty's shoulder. "I shall call you *Mother* instead."

END

ABOUT THE AUTHOR

Vera Day is an avid reader and a joyful writer. After decades coasting along as a lukewarm Christian, and after a few more years of writing in a secular genre under a different pen name, she experienced a series of events that can only be described as epiphanic... in the God sense, not the light bulb sense, though that also applies.

Now Vera Day writes in a new genre, the faith-inspired cozy mystery.

Vera lives in small-town Texas with her two-legged and four-legged family members. Her neighbor is a cow, but as far as neighbors go, Daisy is a good 'un!

When Did We Lose Sylvia? is Vera's first cozy mystery novel.

Printed in Great Britain
by Amazon